D0873130
Woof Woof Story
I TOLD YOU TO TURN ME INTO A Pampered Pooch, NOT FENRIR!
Inumajin
ILLUSTRATION BY
Kochimo

Contents

Len
Her true identity is the blue dragon Lenowyrm. Having fallen for Routa, she assumes the form of a mouse and lives in his fur.
Routa
He was supposed to be reincarnated as a normal dog, but he's unmistakably Fenrir. Nevertheless, he commits himself to the dog act and lives his pet life to the fullest.
Toa
One of the mansion's few apprentice maids. She is terrified of Routa.
Miranda
Mary's personal maid and Toa's senior.
Mary
Routa's owner. She spoils him rotten with love and affection.

Hecate
A beautiful witch who lives in the forest.
Nahura
Hecate's familiar.

Woof Woof Story
I TOLD YOU TO TURN ME INTO A
Pampered Pooch,
NOT FENRIR!

Inumajin
ILLUSTRATION BY
Kochimo

Woof Woof Story

I TOLD YOU TO TURN ME INTO A *Pampered Pooch*, NOT FENRIR!

VOLUME 2

Inumajin

Translation by Jennifer O'Donnell
Cover art by Kochimo

Yen On
1290 Avenue of the Americas
New York, NY 10104

Visit us at yenpress.com

facebook.com/yenpress
twitter.com/yenpress

yenpress.tumblr.com
instagram.com/yenpress

First Yen On Edition: June 2019

Yen On is an imprint of Yen Press, LLC.
The Yen On name and logo are trademarks of Yen Press, LLC.

The publisher is not responsible for websites (or their content) that are not owned by the publisher.

Library of Congress Cataloging-in-Publication Data
Names: Inumajin, author. | Kochimo, illustrator. | O'Donnell, Jennifer, translator.
Title: Woof woof story : I told you to turn me into a pampered pooch, not fenrir! / Inumajin ; illustration by Kochimo ; translation by Jennifer O'Donnell ; cover art by Kochimo.
Other titles: Wanwan Monogatari. English | I told you to turn me into a pampered pooch, not fenrir!
Description: First Yen On edition. | New York, NY : Yen On, 2018–
Identifiers: LCCN 2018051028 | ISBN 9781975303181 (v. 1 : pbk.) | ISBN 9781975303204 (v. 2 : pbk.)
Subjects: CYAC: Reincarnation—Fiction. | Wishes—Fiction. | Dogs—Fiction. | Fantasy.
Classification: LCC PZ7.1.I63 Wo 2018 | DDC [Fic]—dc23
LC record available at https://lccn.loc.gov/2018051028

ISBNs: 978-1-9753-0320-4 (paperback)
978-1-9753-0321-1 (ebook)

1 3 5 7 9 10 8 6 4 2

LSC-C

Printed in the United States of America

High above the spot Len and I are taking shade in, a feline voice calls out to us. There, perched on a branch, is a crimson cat with her paws tucked beneath her.

It's Nahura, who forces a "meow" onto the ends of her sentences to make herself seem more catlike.

She's actually a homunculus that's been forced into the body of a cat, but I don't know the details.

She's also a bona fide cat burglar who makes frequent trips to the mansion to steal my food right from my bowl. Truly a formidable foe who has heartlessly gobbled up three entire meals of mine without remorse.

"Woof, woof. *(There's nothing weird about it. If there's a dog, it needs a collar. If there's a collar, it needs a dog. So what's wrong with a pet dog wanting one?)*"

"Squeak. *(But you're a Fen Wolf, not a dog. And you're the alpha wolf, the esteemed king of the Fen Wolves, Fenrir.)*"

"Woof, woof! *(No I'm nooot! I'm a dooog! And even if I* was *a Fen Wolf, I'm still just an adorable puppy.)*"

"Mrow! *(Ah-ha-ha! You're not cute at all!)*"

"Woof! *(Shut up! It's not funny!)*"

My lady calls me cute all the time! Even if no one else does!

"Squeak? *(So? Why do you desire a collar?)*"

"Arwf...... *(Hmph, just listen to this...or, well, watch this.)*"

I move away from the shade of the tree and over to the tiny maid attempting to hang up some wet laundry.

"Hup! Nnf!"

She's not quite tall enough and has to stand on her tiptoes as she tries to hang sheets over the clothesline. Her black hair is done up in pigtails that bob up and down in her struggle, and it's actually pretty adorable.

I wonder if she'll be okay without a stool to stand on. I feel like she's about to miss and drop everything at any moment.

"Arwf, arwf! *(Hey, little maid!)*"

I waltz over and nuzzle up to one of her legs.

"Arww, arww? *(Working hard, I see. Why don't you take a break and pet me?)*"

If this were Lady Mary, she'd be delighted by what I just did, but this maid…

"E-eeeeeeeeek!"

She practically leaps out of her skin and clings to a freshly washed sheet, which then slowly sinks to the ground. The once-clean white sheet is now covered in grass stains.

"A-arwf. *(O-oh no, I'm sorry. I didn't think I'd make you jump that much.)*"

"D-don't come any closer…"

She kicks her legs out, giving the impression of running in place as she's pinned to the ground by fear.

"Arwf. *(Hee-hee. Little girls' crying faces are so cute. I wanna give her a lick.)*"

……Wait, let's forget I said that!

"Bark. *(See my point* now? *This is how people have been reacting to me lately.)*"

At first, it was only a few of the maids, like this one, but more and more people have become wary of me as I've grown.

Papa Gandolf, the master of the house, and Lady Mary seem fine with it, so no one's said anything, but I've felt more and more passing glances that seem to wonder *Is he really a dog?*

And I'm not being overly self-conscious about this.

It's not that every single person here suspects my true identity, but it's clear the oblivious servants are finally starting to open their eyes.

This is bad. Really, really bad.

Not many people still treat me the same as when I first arrived at the mansion. One standout is the chef, old man James.

He still laughs with a "gya-ha-ha" as he pets my head and feeds me delicious food. He's the best. The best of the best.

Actually, I can think of one more person who treats me the same as when I first got here, but she's been trying to eliminate me for as long as I can remember.

"Grrrr……?! *(That's right—the freeloading knight, my rival*

slacker, Zenobia... Doesn't she have anything better to do than test her new blades on me...?!)"

"O-oh no......"

The maid is still looking at me like I'm about to eat her.

Urgh, the fear hurts; it really does.

Sure, she acts like this now, but when I was a lot smaller, she would actually hug me during her work. She even used to bury her face into my fluffy chest.

Those precious memories make her fear sting me that much more.

"Bark, bark! *(It's all because of this stupid Fenrir body! Who would want to have such a terrifying form?! I just wanted to be a dog! A pampered pooch! A lazy dog allowed to get fat off eating too much tasty food! This is all that pretty goddess's fault with her stupid* special service...*!)*"

I glare at the sky, baring my hatred at the useless goddess who reincarnated me.

I can see her now, waving back at me from the blue sky with an ignorant smile.

"Squeak? *(Huh? What's this about a goddess?)*"

"Mewl. *(He's spouting nonsense again. We can probably just ignore it.)*"

Oh yeah, I haven't actually mentioned to anyone that I was reincarnated.

It'd be difficult to explain, and if they don't believe me, they'll just treat me like I'm an idiot. Probably best to let Nahura think whatever she wants.

"WOOF, WOOF!!! *(I may be big and terrifying. It may have been only two months since I was born (LOL). And I might be a dog (temp.). But there exists an item that will take the edge off my frightening look for sure! And that item is a C-O-L-L-A-R!)*"

My desire for a collar is so strong that when I yell, I feel like I'm about to fire another beam.

"Eek! N-noooooo!"

"Squeak. *(You're going to scare the poor girl to death if you continue shouting like that, beloved.)*"

"Arwf…… *(Whoops, sorry about that.)*"

I tamp down an overwhelming desire to lick the trembling young maid who's gripping the sheet.

"Woof, woof. *(Anyway, let me spell it out for you. If there's a dog, it needs a collar. If there's a collar, it needs a dog. Even if the dog's big, they look less intimidating when they have a collar on, right?)*"

As long as I can get a collar, then the little maid and all the other servants will stop being so afraid of me.

Humans are very susceptible to signals. If I have something that clearly marks me as a pet, then I'm sure they'll go back to being oblivious and thinking of me as a harmless pup.

"Squeak. *(No, I don't think that's how it works at all.)*"

"Mewl. *(I can hardly believe a collar will be enough to solve your problems, Routa.)*"

Len looks at me with eyes half-closed and full of doubt. Nahura simply laughs at me.

"WOOF, WOOF! *(Fine! Whatever! I was an idiot for telling you two!)*"

"Ahhh?! Uwah…pleeease… What is *wrong* with you?!"

Oh, crap. I barked too loud again.

Now this tiny maid's gone from teary eyes to outright bawling.

I'm not sure if she managed to shake off the fear, but she snaps back at me a little.

That's super-cute, too, little maid. I really wanna lick you.

"Squeak… *(This is moronic… I shall return to my slumber.)*"

"Mewl. *(I'm going to find a patch of sun to lie in.)*"

Len burrows into my mane, and Nahura leaves to find a sunny spot.

Which leaves me alone with the sniffling maid.

How am I supposed to comfort her? I'm pretty sure she'll just cry more if I lick her. Maybe I'd be better off not doing anything at all…

But just as I think that, a petite silhouette approaches through the curtains of sheets.

"Roouutaa! Where are you?"

Wha—?! Is that Lady Mary?!

"Oh, there you are. Bad Routa, you shouldn't get in the way of Toa's work—"

My lady's head pops out from between the white sheets.

She's the very picture of a perfect young maiden, with her light-blond hair and deep-blue eyes. And her smile is just for me.

Ooh, she's super-cute today as well. Super-duper-cute.

But her lovely expression quickly darkens.

"Routa…? What are—?"

U-uh-oh. She's definitely the type to misunderstand this scene!

The crumpled maid, crying as she grips the sheets. And me, howling wildly in front of her.

It certainly looks like I'm five seconds away from attacking her.

And that's the only part of this whole interaction that she saw! The only logical explanation is—a dangerous beast?! Extermination?!

"Arww, arww! *(I-i-it's not what it looks like, my lady! I wasn't going to do anything! I was just rubbing against the back of her knees and got excited by the maid's crying!)*"

Okay, that would be a major crime if I were a human, but I'm a pet, so it's fine! There's no problem at all!

"What did you do to Toa? You shouldn't make her cry! Bad dog!"

She puts a hand on her waist and raises the index finger of her other hand to scold me.

She is not scary at all, just incredibly cute. My lady is always super-cute.

"Honestly, don't you wag your tail so much. This is a scolding, understand, Routa? Bad dog! Bad dog!"

"Bark, bark! *(Yes! Thank you! I have turned over a new paw!)*"

Lady Mary puffing out her cheeks is even cuter. My wagging tail picks up speed.

Apparently, the black-haired pigtailed maid is called Toa. I'll remember that.

"Oh, Toa! What are you doing in front of the young lady…?!"

Following behind Lady Mary is the maid Miranda, who is shocked by the sight in front of her.

The freshly washed sheets are now covered in grass and mud. They're going to have to be rewashed.

"Ah, um, this is…er…"

The confused Toa gropes for an answer. She's probably going to be punished.

I can't let that happen! Especially when it's all my fault… But there's no way for Toa to talk her way out of this one.

Guess there's only one thing I can do.

"I-I'm sorry, Miranda; I—"

"Woof! *(Hyup!)*"

I leap at Toa as she bolts to her feet.

"Ahhh! Ahhhhh— Huh?"

My target isn't Toa, but the sheets she's holding.

"Arwwwf! *(Mwa-ha-ha-ha! I'll take this! And this!)*"

I drape them over my head and hold them in my mouth as I roll around on the ground, increasing the sheets' filth levels a good 300 percent.

"Ahhh!"

Miranda takes one look at the grass-covered sheets, her mouth agape, and immediately, her anger turns to me.

"Routa! You've gone too far this time! I shall speak to chef James, and you'll certainly go without dinner tonight!"

"A-arwf?! *(Huh? Wait!* That's *my punishment?! Don't take my dinner awaaaay! Not when I'm still growiiiing!)*"

I drop the sheets, fold my ears back, and lie on the ground.

I forgot. Miranda is the only servant who isn't scared of me at all.

"Arww, arww! *(I'm sorry! Please! Don't do that!)*"

"Miranda… It looks like Routa's sorry, so maybe you can forgive him this time?"

Oh, my lady is so kind. What an angel.

I nuzzle Lady Mary as she wraps herself around my neck and vouches for me.

"…Very well, then. Please excuse me, my lady."

Miranda sighs and picks up the dirt-covered sheets.

"I shall rewash these, Toa; you finish hanging up the rest of the sheets."

"Y-yes, ma'am!"

Her pigtails bob as Toa retrieves the remaining sheets from the wash basket.

There, that should keep Toa from getting in trouble.

"Let's go play over there so you don't get in the way again."

"Woof! *(Yeah! I'd love to!)*"

I follow after my lady to the middle of the garden, my tail wagging all the while.

I see Toa pause her sheet-hanging duties, and it looks like she's about to say something.

But I'm sure I'll just scare her again if I approach her.

I think nothing of it as I choose to follow my lady instead.

"Come on, Routa!"

"Bark! *(Let's do this!)*"

After we play fetch in the garden, we enjoy some tea and light reading in the shade of a tree. Refreshed after her break, Lady Mary returns to her afternoon studies.

Mission complete.

...Oh, wait, the collar.

† † †

"Really, Father?!"

It's evening, and I'm relaxing in the living room when I hear my lady's voice.

"Arwf?! *(Huh, what's going on?!)*"

Dozing off by the fire, I suddenly snap my head up in surprise.

Maybe it's because the mountains are so close, but while the afternoons are nice and warm, the mornings and evenings get pretty chilly.

Listening to the sound of kindling crackle as I loaf to my heart's content is the best.

"Yes, I can combine this with some business I have in the imperial capital, but I shall have a few days free. We can take our time traveling there first, though."

"Oh, how wonderful! Thank you so much, Father!"

"Great, I've already summoned the ship. It will be the perfect way to celebrate your return to health, Mary."

Lady Mary is now in perfect health thanks to the wyrmnil we took from Len's nest. Papa must also think it's a good idea for her to have a break from her daily studies and enjoy a chance to spread her wings a bit.

"Arwf? *(Still, what does he mean, 'ship'? Are we close to the ocean?)*"

I was brought to this mansion soon after I was born, so I have no knowledge of the surrounding area. The only geography I'm familiar with is the enormous forest to the north of the mansion and the waterfall even farther north of that. That's where Len used to live.

"Routa! This'll be our first journey together! I can't wait!"

"Arwf! *(You're taking me, too? Yippee!)*"

I wonder if I'll get to try the beds and cuisine of the imperial capital.

I don't want to do anything but eat and sleep, even on vacation. Just one of my lazy-dog qualities.

"If that's the case, then please allow me to accompany you!"

A knight, gripping the hilt of her sword, pipes up.

She has smart features, and her hair, a fiery crimson, is tied up in a ponytail. This is none other than Zenobia Lionheart. Or as I like to call her, the no-good knight.

She had been standing motionless, playing bodyguard next to the door, but is now suddenly speaking right at Papa's side.

"I am responsible for your safety as well as the young lady's! Please allow me to continue carrying out my duties!"

"O-of course. You're welcome to come along as my guest, but please, there's no need to get so worked up, though your diligence is appreciated. It is certainly reassuring that the knight who defeated a dragon will be protecting us."

"Oh, well, that dragon incident was, um..."

Whenever the dragon's defeat is mentioned, Zenobia instantly clams up.

Well, all she did was ransack the place. To be honest, her only contribution was sucker punching the dragon who wanted to resolve everything peacefully, which in turn pissed it off, and so the dragon ended up beating her within an inch of her life. But if Zenobia hadn't said she defeated the dragon, then everyone would be suspicious of my true identity. That's why everyone thinks she's a hero now.

"Grrr..."

Zenobia glares at me as I chuckle internally.

Ha-ha-ha! That frustrated expression is the best. I seriously have to lick her someday.

"So when do we leave, Father?"

"Oh, tomorrow."

Lady Mary's expression freezes upon hearing his response.

"Wh-why didn't you tell me sooner?! I have to get ready! Please help me, Miranda!"

"Yes, my lady. There's no need to worry, though. We have plenty of time. Just leave it to us."

Miranda smiles as she tries to calm her down, chasing after her mistress who's just flown out of the room. She doesn't look fazed at all.

Seeing how Miranda kept a level head in such a situation reminds me of exactly how incredible the servants of this household really are.

"I thought she was still a child, but it seems Mary truly is becoming a lady. It sure takes a while for a woman to prepare her things."

Papa Gandolf has come over to pet my head.

"Arwf! *(You're right. That's something men just don't understand. Although, now that I'm in this body, it has even less to do with me!)*"

I'm getting more and more excited about this sudden vacation.

I think the last trip I took in my old life was a field trip during high school. My existence back then was even more miserable than you could imagine.

Guess I'll try to enjoy this vacation with Lady Mary the best I can.

That evening, my lady struggles to stay awake as she works with the maids to decide what clothing and other travel essentials she'll take with her.

The moon is high in the sky by the time she finally goes to bed.

"Phew… Routa…I can't wait to leave tomorrow……"

"Arww. *(Yep, yep. Same. Which means we should get to sleep ASAP so we don't have trouble waking up tomorrow.)*"

I've grown so big that even this luxurious canopy bed feels pretty small. These days, Lady Mary has to sleep holding on to me.

She presses her face into my fluffy body and soon drifts off into slumber.

"*Yaaaawn. (I should sleep, too… Good night, my lady.)*"

With thoughts of tomorrow's trip buzzing in my mind, I let out a big yawn and fall asleep in no time.

The Faulks family mansion is so extravagant, you could easily mistake it for a castle, so of course the land surrounding it is appropriately massive.

Especially the garden, which is larger than my middle school was.

It's not just large, though—it sports an elaborate layout.

The talented gardener has worked his magic, so the lush lawn has no odd gaps anywhere. Each and every blade of grass rises to the same height. The emerald expanse is trimmed so cleanly that it resembles green carpeting.

In the center is a water fountain with white stone paths branching off in all directions, and along each path are flower arrangements with various themes that any passerby can enjoy.

It's a garden absolutely rich with character. *Filthy rich,* in fact.

And above this garden—one of the many treasures of the household—is…

"Arwwwwwwwwf! *(It's huuuuuuge!)*"

...a giant ship floating in the air.

The immense vessel hovers in place, its sheer size creating eddies in the air as a light breeze passes by.

I look up at this incredible sight, mouth agape.

"Arwf...! *(Papa said he called a ship, but I never would've guessed it'd be an airship...!)*"

But even if I call it an airship, this thing is nothing like the blimps that are just a passenger compartment attached to a gigantic balloon. If anything, it looks more like a sailboat.

It's made with subdued dark-brown wood and has a female figurehead mounted on the prow, most likely for good luck while flying.

The more I stare at the sculpture, the more it resembles the goddess who had me reincarnated into this life... Do the people of this world worship her?

"Woof, woof! *(Wait, how is this thing floating? Must be magic. Man, this stuff is incredible. You really can do anything with magic, huh? I mean, this ship is insanely huge!)*"

I've seen both Nahura and her master, Hecate, use magic that can make things levitate, but this is on a completely different level.

"Oh-ho, does this ship pique your interest, Routa?"

My mouth is still wide open when Papa asks me this.

"This is a large airship that my company, Faulks Co., developed. This one is the flagship, the *Jeremiah*."

Papa strokes his beard with pride.

"This ship was built using techniques developed by the imperial capital's Institute of Magical Research. It's outfitted with four giant magical Flo Ruu furnaces, each equipped with six exhausts. That means it can fly quietly for long distances at incredible speeds. I plan to put them into service next spring, but I've borrowed this vessel under the pretense of a trial run. Right now, this high-speed ship is only meant to entertain the royal aristocracy, but I'd like to produce more someday, bring the cost down, and use these for intercontinental transport of goods and people. But there are a mountain of issues concerning weather, international borders, flying monsters—"

He's acting like a child who's proud of his toy as he speaks about it at great length, but unfortunately, all this info goes in one ear and out the other.

"Arwf, arwf. *(Ohhh, uh-huh, wow. I see. Ohhh, uh-huh, wow. I see.)*"

"As expected, Routa, you understand my vision."

"Arwf. *(Nope, I wasn't able to follow any of that. Not a word. I just know that this ship is* amaaaazing.*)*"

Wait. Does that mean this ship is Papa's? This ridiculously huge flying ship is his personal aircraft?

Whoa, Papa's incredible. Or at least, this family's wealth is incredible.

"Father! Father!"

Lady Mary is waiting behind us, but the moment he stops talking, she tugs on his sleeve.

"Oh, of course. Let's continue this conversation on board. Shall we?"

On the side of the ship is the gangway. There are a number of slanting ladders that the servants had been using to carry the luggage on board.

""""Safe travels, Master and Lady Mary.""""

The servants seeing us off all speak in unison as they bow together in a single movement.

Only a few maids are accompanying us on this trip to attend to Papa and Lady Mary, with Miranda in charge. But that doesn't mean that everyone else stayed behind because they think I'm too scary, right?

That can't be it, right?! They just didn't want to impose, right?!

"Take care, now!"

Just behind the servants is old man James. His chef's hat is off as he waves.

He works in the mansion as part of the kitchen staff, but he's also Papa's personal friend, meaning he's not really a servant.

Papa invited him to come along on our journey, but James is really busy and turned him down. Papa seemed dejected about the whole thing, but I was even more disappointed. I'll have to spend an entire journey without the old man's cooking!

I could eat five—no, ten—of his meals per day easily, and now I have to go who-knows-how-long without it…

"Arwf! *(Well then, we'll just have to see how skilled the chefs of the capital are! I'll test it all myself!)*"

I'm sure Papa will treat me! He'll make sure I get to eat amazing food while we're there! Papa's definitely going to treat me!

"Hey, don't get so excited just because this is your first journey. If you try anything weird when we get there, you'll cause problems for the master and the young lady."

Zenobia, who has volunteered to act as their bodyguard on this trip, speaks to me in a low voice.

We shared the highs and lows of an adventure when we went to find the wyrmnil, but her attitude toward me hasn't softened at all.

I'm still on edge around her, as per usual. The constant bloodlust she has for me makes my skin crawl.

She's always staring when I'm playing with Lady Mary in the shade of a tree, always outside the bath when we're bathing, always watching me when I'm napping while my lady studies.

What is she? A stalker? Is she actually in love with me or something?

I hound Zenobia as she continues to eye me with suspicion.

"Woof? *(Hey, Zenobia, before you start worrying about me, how about you make sure you don't get lost on* this *trip as well, hmm?)*"

She has zero sense of direction, after all.

If she loses her way in the chaotic streets of the big city, she'll be scarred for life.

"Wh-why are you looking at me like that? Are you implying I've done something wrong?"

"Arwf… *(Nah, sorry for getting worked up, but I'm getting the distinct feeling you might screw up at another critical juncture…)*"

"Tch… I may have been unconscious during the fight with the

dragon, but you won't be the hero again this time. I'll be the one who protects the master and young lady…!"

"Arwf. *(Yeah, well, I'm just a pet, so being asked to help protect anyone is a little ridiculous. I'll leave everything to you, so have fun working and being useful for once.)*"

If she can't do her job at a time like this, who knows if she'll ever manage.

On the other hand, I don't feel a lick of guilt for taking it easy right now!

Because I'm a pet! Pampered pooch life is the best!

"Let's go, Routa! We'll be the first ones on board!"

After my lady curtsies for the captain as he greets his passengers, she rushes over to the ship's gangway.

Hmm, even though she looks so prim and proper, she really is a bit of a tomboy. Then again, that's something I find absolutely adorable about her.

"My lady! Wait for me! I shall accompany you!"

Zenobia chases after her.

"Woof, woof! *(Lady Mary! Wait!)*"

She'll get lost if you go too far ahead! Seriously, Zenobia gets easily confused! I just know she'll get lost if you leave her behind! Wait! For real, wait up!

"Come on, Routa, hurry up."

"Woof, woof! *(You're too fast, my lady!)*"

I try as hard as I can to keep pace with her spirited sprinting. The ship is fairly large, but it's still cramped for my giant body. The moment I pass by crew members, they turn to look at me and then turn right back around. I don't know if they were told about me in advance, but for whatever reason, they're not freaking out.

Sorry, crew. I'm sure it's a shock to see something as huge as me running around your ship.

"I found stairs, Routa! Let's go take a look!"

"Arwf. *(Come on, Lady Mary, how are you so energetic? We got on board like two minutes ago.)*"

We explore the ship to her heart's content until I have no idea where we are anymore.

When we peek into the engine room, someone shows us the gem-like crystals used to power the ship; and on the bridge, the captain lets Lady Mary wear his captain's hat and touch the steering wheel. I feel like we've explored just about every nook and cranny.

But then we find ourselves at the royal suite.

Of course, there's a restaurant, but there's also a bar and an area that looks like a theater.

This incredibly luxurious cruise ship is something Papa's extremely proud of. And it's easy to see why. I always dreamed of going on a cruise like this in my past life... Wait, no. No sad thoughts allowed. I don't want to ruin this happy moment.

...Hmm. Where's Zenobia?

I guess we did end up leaving her behind, earlier. She couldn't keep up with our exploration.

I'm sure our knight has assumed some kind of fervent duty to find Lady Mary, whom she no doubt believes is now missing somewhere on the ship. But, of course, it's Zenobia who's actually lost.

The pleasant sound of my lady's shoes clicking against the ground cuts through the air.

We continue to climb some stairs, and I spot an exit. A blinding white light fills my vision, we step outside, and—

"Woooow...!"

My lady cries out in wonder.

We're graced by the sight of a gorgeous blue sky just above a sea of clouds.

"Arwf! *(Whoa! Amazing! What a spectacular view!)*"

So this is the deck? We reached the highest part of the ship in no time at all.

But man, is this view incredible.

I look up to see a rich blue sky. Then look down to see an ocean of fluffy white clouds expanding below me.

"Arwf… *(I flew on planes a number of times for work in my past life, but I never thought there would be this much of a difference seeing the sky like* this *instead of through a window…)*"

The view stretching 360 degrees around me is breathtaking. Completely different from the narrow perspective you get in economy class.

The airship sails through the sky, cutting through the clouds like waves.

"It's so beautiful…"

My lady rests one hand on the deck's railing and uses the other to hold down her hair billowing in the wind as she enjoys the vista of the sky.

"Woof. *(Posing that way makes you look like you're in a painting, my lady.)*"

Even the most famous works of art don't hold a candle to this scene. I wish I could save this image and keep it forever. If I had a camera, I'd take as many pictures as possible.

Ahhh, she's so beautiful.

"Arw? *(Huh? That's weird.)*"

We're at a crazy-high altitude, but the air isn't thin. It's not freezing cold out, either. Just a little nippy against my skin.

"That's because of a contract made with the wind spirits who have put a barrier to block the air outside."

"Arwf! *(I know that voice…!)*"

It's a woman's voice, and it's so bewitching that anyone hearing it would go weak in the knees.

"Dr. Hecate!"

"That took you a while. I was getting tired of waiting."

Standing there is a beautiful woman with a wide-brimmed witch hat and a glass of liquor in one hand.

"Woof, woof. *(Oh, it's you, Hecate. I didn't know you were on board.)*"

"Ha-ha, I am Mary's attending physician, after all. It's my duty to monitor my patient's progress after administering treatment."

"I'm already back to full health! And it's all thanks to your medicine!"

"Oh my, you need not thank *me*... Whoops, I shouldn't say anything."

Hecate looks at me with a knowing grin.

Shh! It's a secret! Don't tell Lady Mary anything about who got the medicine!

"Huh? What was that? Something secret? Tell me! Tell me!"

"Hee-hee, no way."

"Aw, you're such a meanie!"

My lady pulls at Hecate's arm playfully.

Hee-hee-hee. Seeing these beautiful women playing really warms my heart.

"It really is wonderful that you can come on this trip with us, Doctor!"

"I have some errands to attend to in the imperial capital, so this was perfect timing. Teleporting in a flash with magic is a rather dull way to travel."

"There you are, Mary. Did you have fun exploring?"

That is when Papa climbs up the stairs. Behind him is a sheepish-looking Zenobia.

Oh-ho, would you look at that? It seems Papa picked up a lost Zenobia on his way over.

"Arwf! *(Hey, look everyone! Zenobia's trash at guard duty!)*"

I stick my tongue out at her in a way that Lady Mary won't see.

"Tch...! Y-you little...!"

"W-woof! Woof! *(Whoa! Hey! You shouldn't draw your sword on a flight! Look, my lady! Look at what she's doing! Hey now! Restrain yourself!)*"

I immediately retreat to Lady Mary's side.

"What's wrong, Routa?"

"Grrr...!"

I knew it—she can't do anything to me when everyone else is around. Zenobia looks at me in frustration as she removes her hand from the hilt of her sword.

"Arwf. *(Ha, I win.)*"

I hide behind Lady Mary, proud of my victory, as Papa's eyes widen in surprise.

"D-Dr. Hecate?! What are you doing here…?! I don't remember contacting you…"

"Oh? It almost sounds like you wish I wasn't here."

"N-no! That's not it at all!"

Papa shakes his head in denial. Even Papa, who's normally so dignified, gets flustered in front of Hecate.

It seems Papa has known her since he was a young man, so it's no mystery that Hecate knows a few ways to push his buttons.

"Gandolf, I do believe this is the first time I've ever been aboard your ship. It's quite magnificent."

"What? Oh right, yes, thank you very much. I'm quite proud of it. It is truly an achievement for the Faulks name."

Papa gives an honest reply to the sudden compliment, albeit in a curious tone.

"I see. I think so, too. By the way, can you remind me of who exactly acted as a mediator, forging the contract with the spirits to erect the air barrier for this fine vessel?"

Hecate gives him a naughty, bewitching grin.

"Th-that was you."

His cheeks flush.

"And who spoke with the famously stubborn Institute of Magical Research?"

"Why, you, of course!"

"And who gave you the crystallization technique for the floating ore that powers this airship?"

"You!"

"That's right. I gave you so much, yet I received no invitation, did I?"

"......!"

Ah, this was a lost cause from the start. Hecate's so deeply involved with the ship's inception that without her, we wouldn't even be here right now.

She's a witch, she's a doctor, *and* she has connections in the imperial capital? Just who is this superwoman? If only she weren't a glutton, or a wine thief, or had a less rotten personality...

Papa is now soaked in a cold sweat as Hecate's smile grows wider.

"Do you have anything to say for yourself?"

"You are welcome to board this ship whenever you please! You are our most esteemed guest!"

"Oh, why, thank you. I'm glad to hear it."

She pulls a complete one-eighty, her evil grin morphing into the gentle smile of a young lady, her hand on one cheek as she takes a sip of her amber drink.

Papa heaves a huge sigh before his eyes move to Hecate's drink.

"B-by the way, Doctor... That drink of yours......"

He lifts a trembling finger and points at the bottle Hecate's waving around.

"Oh, this? It's a fifty-eight-year-old Selenhorun."

She gulps down the last of her glass and sighs with decadent satisfaction.

Then she tilts the bottle and pours herself another.

"That's not what I meant! I was planning to enjoy that on this trip...! Ahhh, you're guzzling such an expensive liquor like water...!"

"Oh? Am I?"

"Yes! Please give it back!"

He shakes his right fist in the air. Confronting Hecate with a look of renewed vigor, he seems determined to get the bottle back, no matter what.

He really, really wants to drink that booze. Actually, I want to try some, too.

"...Hmph."

Hecate narrows her fearless eyes, the glass against her lips.

Uh-oh, she clearly set another trap for him.

"Gandolf, do you remember the results from your last checkup?"

"U-ughhh...!"

Papa's shoulders start to shake in response.

What's this? Does he have some kind of health issue?

"You drink and eat far too much. Don't you remember I told you your uric acid levels are pushing it, putting you at higher risk of gout?"

Pfft! Gout? Papa lives way too extravagantly. But I guess that's what happens when you drink every single night while eating rich, heavy foods like honey-slathered cheese.

No, I shouldn't be laughing. It actually sounds like a serious issue. I've never had it, so I don't actually know what gout entails, but judging by the name, maybe simply going outside is painful.

"I even recommended you food to remedy it. And I told you to cut back on the alcohol."

"You did..."

Papa trembles, sweating so aggressively that I'm worried he might get dehydrated.

"Then what's this? What is this alcohol doing here? There's even plenty left in the cellar. Gandolf, have you been secretly snacking on fatty foods and drinking behind my back?"

"N-n-no, o-of course... Yes, I have."

"Do you regret it now?"

"Yes..."

"No more drinking, then. Agreed?"

"Yes......"

"Good. I will, though."

"......Please have as much as you like......"

Papa breaks down, a flood of tears streaming down his face.

So that's why Hecate always comes to the mansion and helps herself to a bunch of his alcohol.

"Mmm, mmm. This really is delicious."

Or not. I have no doubt that she just wants to get drunk on somebody else's dime.

"Uwah...ungh... Just when I finally got my hands on it......"

Papa's really bawling now. He's a little too comfortable looking pathetic around his daughter. He has the distinguished presence of a silver fox, but he's also a bit too fragile.

"Father..."

His face is such a mess from crying that my lady hands him a handkerchief.

"Father. I'm feeling a bit thirsty. Would you like to have some tea with me?"

"Oh, Mary......"

She's trying to cheer her father up since he can't have alcohol anymore. She must be an angel. No, she literally is an angel. There's no mistaking it. She's my little angel.

She leads Papa, who's so touched that he starts sobbing yet again, away to the rear of the deck.

"Woof, woof! *(I'm coming, too! Maybe I'll swipe some desserts.)*"

Just as I start setting off after them in excitement, I feel something scampering around the scruff of my neck.

"Squeak...? *(What is the meaning of this commotion...?)*"

"Arwf? *(Oh, did you* just *wake up?)*"

The face of a sleepy blue mouse pops up from my fluffy mane. Her eyes widen at the sight of the new scenery.

"Squee?! *(Wh-whaaaaaaaat?! Why are we in the aiiiiiiir?! Where are weeeeeeee?!)*"

"Arwf?! *(You're kidding, right?! How long have you been asleep?!)*"

Come to think of it, I hadn't heard a squeak out of her since midday yesterday.

Did she really sleep for a good twenty-four hours? There is such a thing as *too* much sleep. What a perfect recluse.

Damn it, I feel like I'm losing!

"Squeak, squeak. *(Small matter... I exist to soar above the clouds.*

My hunger is a far more pressing concern. Perhaps you can explain our current situation while preparing a meal.)"

"Woof, woof! *(Pipe down! You're so demanding for a squatter. Dessert crumbs from teatime are good enough for you.)*"

"Squee? *(Oh, dessert? Very well. I am fond of sweet things.)*"

Tch. Nothing discourages her…!

"Woof! *(Argh! Fine, then. I'm sure you know this already, but don't peek out from my fur.)*"

No matter how you look at her, she clearly looks like a mouse.

Do you have any idea how terrifying a cook is when they see a mouse?

"Squee. *(Very well. I shall not jeopardize your social standing. I am a woman who stands by her husband.)*"

"Woof, woof? *(Who're you calling your husband? For starters, both parties need to consent to marriage.)*"

Not to mention there's a humongous gap in our species and ages.

A wife and kids? *No thank you.* I don't need that ball and chain.

My ideal life is to be a pet.

Ohhh, how I would love to be Lady Mary's pet for the rest of my life. I want her to spoil me and pamper me. Sorry, Len, but I'd rather die than be some dragon's husband.

"Woof. *(I only remembered after you popped up, but it seems like Nahura's not around.)*"

If Hecate's here then that means Nahura should be, too, or rather, she should have been dragged along, as well.

"Squee. *(Hee-hee. That means I get you all to myself.)*"

"Arwf. *(Uh-huh, sure, good for you.)*"

"Squee! *(You're no fun at all! Meanie! Prepare yourself!)*"

As Len and I exchange banter, I walk over to the consulting room where Lady Mary and the others have retired, and there I see—

"Mewl. *(You're late, Routa. This dessert is delectable, by the way.)*"

Nahura is getting nice and cozy in the warm room, enjoying some dessert.

"Mrow? *(What's with the scary face? Oh, sorry. You always look like that.)*"

She lifts a paw to her mouth and chuckles, her cheeks stuffed with sweets.

"Woof? *(So where is this delectable dessert, then?)*"

"......Mew? *(......Hmm? Well, that's strange. There doesn't seem to be any more.)*"

"Woof! Woof! *(What's strange is your extreme gluttonyyyy!)*"

I knock her over with my paws.

"Arwf. *(Oh-ho, not bad.)*"

I appraise the evening meal as a helping is piled high on a plate.

"And here we have our main course, flying fish à la meunière. Some crew members who had a bit of extra time on their hands fished these fresh from the clouds as we came to collect you."

"Ha-ha-ha, I see you've inherited your master's love of fishing."

"Arwf, arwf? *(Ha-ha-ha, is that so?)*"

I can hear the chef explaining how they sourced the ingredients. I'm casually inserting myself into the conversation, but he's actually talking to Papa and the others in the room next door.

"Arww. *(I'm so lonely,* sniff.*)*"

Then again, I'm nothing but a freeloader, so it makes sense I never get to eat with other people. Plus, I'm really loud when I eat, which they think is bad manners. Especially the maids. But that's just how I show my appreciation for the food! A pet has no use for the polite table manners of the upper class. Diving into a meal headfirst is how I do things!

Oh, by the way, it seems the flying fish of this world are fantastical creatures that can actually soar through the sky. To be fair, flying fish in my old world can fly (glide, technically) for up to five hundred meters.

"Arwf... *(...That's pretty fantastical in its own way.)*"

Flying fish are amazing.

But what's *really* amazing is this smell!

Covered in wheat flour and fried. That's all *meunière* means. But don't underestimate its potential.

The rich smell of butter and fat tells my nose this dish contains extraordinary levels of umami.

"Arwf! *(Just look at it. See how it glistens?!)*"

The fish, thrice scored to let the flavor seep in, looks plump and tender, like the juices will ooze out with even the lightest of pokes.

Even at a glance, I can tell that the fried fish skin, liberally seasoned with exotic spices, will be unbelievably crispy.

The fins of the fish, which closely resemble wings, have been fried to perfection and now sit alongside the meunière as a side snack.

The chef is definitely someone who doesn't like to waste a single ingredient. This reminds me of old man James's handiwork.

"Arwf… *(It's too much; I can't resist…)*"

I can't hold back anymore. It's time to dig in!!

I open wide, downing a whole portion in one bite.

The moment the crispy flakes come off, a rich umami spills out and—

"Arwwf?! *(H-how is it soooo gooooooood?!)*"

The fat! It doesn't feel thick or heavy at all! The texture is so light, I'm afraid the fish will fly away. And the amazing fragrance of this butter is filling my nose. How can something taste this gooooood?!

"Mewl! *(Wow! This is scrumptiooooouuuus!)*"

"Squee! *(Whoooaaaa, this is really something!)*"

Nahura and Len appear out of nowhere, trying the meunière from *my* plate.

But they're not wrong. It's delicious. The light, snappy crunch of the outside and soft, melt-in-your-mouth inside complement each other spectacularly.

And the fried fins have been served with a tart tomato sauce that, when eaten after the meunière, tastes very clean and refreshing, and makes you feel like you could eat it forever.

It's incredible. A+.

"Mmm, this is delicious. I see you've gotten even better. Maybe even close to surpassing your master?"

I can hear Papa's high-spirited chortle.

"Not at all. I haven't even come close to half of the master's skill."

"Hmph, I think this meunière could easily compete against something of James's, but I suppose the culinary road is a long one."

I can imagine Papa offering a sage nod.

Color me surprised, though. Seems like the chef who cooked this meunière is one of old man James's students. No wonder it's so tasty.

"Which reminds me, Lord Faulks. How is my master doing? I haven't received a single letter from him, although, I'm sure you know what he's like..."

"Oh, he's doing very well. Can't you tell? He's been having a lot of fun coming up with new recipes for the newest member of our family."

"Ah yes, your massive white dog... He is a dog, correct?"

Yes, I'm a dog! I'm a cute, fluffy puppy! As the old man's student, please inherit some of his obliviousness!

"Yes, his name's Routa. It's quite the challenge keeping his appetite satisfied, which I think is why James enjoys coming up with new menus every day."

"I'm glad to hear it... I do regret that there are techniques he was never able to finish teaching me, but I'm happy that he's happy. If that had never happened, I think he would be the royal chef by now."

"Well, I think punching a member of the royal family was going a bit much. The only thing he could do was lie low in my mansion before he got caught."

"Arwwf?! *(Pfffft! He did* what*?!)*"

There's a limit to how eccentric you can be. Wouldn't doing something like that pretty much guarantee capital punishment?

"Mewl! *(Ew! That's gross! Gross!)*"

Whoops, sorry.

"Squee... *(Honestly, such terrible manners. Here, let me wipe your mouth... Arghhh, I can't... I can't reach it at all...)*"

Wow, old man James is incredible. He's so good, he's even cooked for royalty.

I could tell right from the start that he was someone special!

"*I thought the commotion would have died down by now, so I invited him along. But he refused my invitation. He said he was busy crafting a new recipe and tending to his fields.*"

"*Ha-ha-ha, that sure sounds like him.*"

Seems like the old man's always been that way.

I guess he's always true to himself no matter where he ends up.

"Look at that, Routa. The moon's so big and beautiful..."

It could be argued that this is the best bed a guest could hope for, but it's definitely cramped compared with my lady's extravagant furnishings back home.

It's so small that there isn't enough room to turn over with me in it, but Lady Mary doesn't mind as she squeezes in close to me.

"Arwf. *(Yes, it's a wonderful full moon.)*"

The scene outside the circular guestroom window has a completely different appeal from the splendid view we saw during the day.

The sea of clouds reflecting the brilliant-white glow of the moonlight really is a lovely sight that I wouldn't have gotten to see in my old world. Ah, it makes me want to howl.

It's all thanks to my lady and everyone in the Faulks household that I can enjoy this perfect moment.

If I had remained as my old self, an emotionless drone who died of overwork without any friends or family, then I would have never been able to see and experience this scenery.

I'm so incredibly happy, in a way I've never been able to think about before. I will do anything to protect this life.

Oh, except work, of course.

I renew my vow as I fall asleep with Lady Mary by my side.

02 Sightseeing in the Royal Capital! ...Or So I Thought, but I Found Something Weird!

The next day, the airship descends onto the ocean next to the Royal Capital. We slowly approach the glistening water reflecting the sun's light.

The landing is so gentle, I barely feel it, but the airship is still so huge it creates a splash as waves ripple along the water's surface.

"*Achoo! (Uwah! The spray! It went right up my nose! My eyes sting!)*"

The sea assaults my face.

Trying to catch the moment we touched down on the water was a bad idea.

"Oh, honestly, Routa."

Lady Mary chuckles at me while I try to wipe my face.

Hee-hee-hee. Her smiling face is always adorable. I want to nuzzle my face against hers.

"Mewl! *(Oh, Routa, you're so bad at cleaning your face!)*"

Nahura expertly licks her paw and cleans her own fur.

"Arwf. *(Well, I can't move like a cat.)*"

We're fundamentally different in every way.

I shake the water out of my fur, put my forepaws up on the railing, and gaze at the view in front of me.

"Arwooo!! *(Amaaaazing!!)*"

The white walls of the Royal Capital expand as far as the eye can see. The castle walls between the blue sky and the ocean shine so white that they're blinding. The walls encircle an immense piece of land, apparently designed to fend off invaders even if they aren't approaching from the water.

I wonder if they were built like this due to the threat of monsters in this world.

There's a giant building right in the middle. I'm guessing that's the king's castle.

Having the castle in the center of a town protected by a majestic wall is totally what I'd expect from a place called the Royal Capital.

"Arwf. *(That really is incredible. I'm glad I came.)*"

Our airborne journey comes to an end, and the airship has officially made port in the Royal Capital.

It was almost an entire day from the mansion, but it was so calming, I wish we could have ridden on the ship longer.

I'm looking forward to you taking us home, *Jeremiah.*

"Bark, bark! *(But now it's time for sightseeing in the Royal Capital!)*"

Once the ship arrives in the port, we disembark and get into carriages that will take us to the inn.

"Arwg… *(Urgh, it's cramped in here…)*"

The carriages prepared for us are completely different from the mansion's; they're much smaller. They're supposed to be for four people, but it's not even big enough for me to turn around in. My muzzle and glorious tail stick out the windows.

I lock eyes with the top hat–wearing driver. He forces a smile and then tries to hide his face as much as possible. That's not very nice.

"Well, it shouldn't take too long to reach the inn. Please be patient."

Papa, who's sitting across from me, strokes my head.

It's me, him, and my lady riding together in this carriage. The other two carriages have Hecate, Zenobia, and the maids. The three carriages line up before they start moving, the horses' hooves clopping against the stone road.

"Arwf… *(Wow, this city is the spitting image of Western Europe.)*"

There are people everywhere, and each shop looks prosperous. There are so many people, but the streets aren't dirty at all. That's the center of the kingdom for you. They definitely pay attention to the infrastructure here.

"This area is close to the uptown district where the nobles and aristocrats live. The neighborhoods around the wall are completely different. There are unsavory areas, too. I trust you understand this already, but you shouldn't wander off aimlessly. If you must venture into the city, be sure to have Miranda or Zenobia accompany you."

"Yes, Father."

My lady agrees to Papa's conditions, and he nods with a grunt before the carriage groans to a halt.

It stops in front of the massive gate of a stone building. This must be where Papa is meeting his business associate.

"Well, it's off to work I go. I don't think I'll have any free time until my business has concluded, but I'm hoping everything won't take longer than one day. Then we can spend the remainder of our trip together, just the two of us."

"But, Father, Routa's family, too."

"Ah yes, of course. Just the three of us, then."

"And Zenobia and Miranda. They're important family members, too."

"Ha-ha-ha, so it will be the same as always, then."

"What's wrong with that? I like it when we're all together."

Lady Mary squeezes my neck as she lectures Papa. His eyes crinkle as he pats my head and hers as well.

A pet like me is thrilled to be included. I nuzzle Lady Mary's face in appreciation.

Papa gets out of the carriage, attended by two maids who silently stand behind him.

With that, some men come flying from the gate, flustered.

"Welcome, welcome! Thank you for coming all this way, Lord Gandolf Von Faulks! We're terribly sorry for being so late to meet you! I am Henry Morgan, representative of the Morgan Company!"

"Hmm, it is nothing to concern yourself with. It was my fault for being early. I look forward to working with you today."

So this chubby guy is the person Papa came to see? He's an older gentleman with a pair of eye-catching curly sideburns. His enthusiasm and the way he's rubbing his hands together seem to mark him as a minor player.

"Thank you for your consideration. I hope we will have fruitful negotiations."

"Yes, indeed! You are ever a man of integrity, Lord Von Faulks! I have great admiration for you as a fellow merchant! I never thought I would be in business with the great Faulks Co.; it truly is a dream come true, indeed!"

I don't know if Papa's words are getting through to him, but this Morgan fellow keeps showering him with praise.

Just look at the speed of that hand-wringing! He's going to start a fire if he keeps rubbing them together like that!

From this one conversation, it's pretty easy to see who holds all the cards in this negotiation.

"Woof, woof! *(Good luck, Papa!)*"

The sight of Papa's back as he goes off to work is magnificent! Work hard to fund my livelihood, okay?

"L-Lord Gandolf?! What is that creature?!"

The curly-sideburns man is taken aback by my head sticking out of the carriage window.

"Hmm? Oh, that's my family's dog. He's cute, is he not?"

"D-dog?! That's a *dog*?!"

"……Yes? Is something the matter?"

"N-no! No, no, no?! Don't be absurd! I merely meant o-of *course* the wonderful Lord Faulks would have such a spectacular dog! To tell you the truth, my daughter is also—"

He may be surprised by the extent of Papa's obliviousness, but the speed at which he switches from surprise to flattery is impressive. When it comes to doing business with a big fish like Papa, you have to start currying favor from the first meeting all the way until the end.

Overlooking that would be shooting yourself in the foot. I can empathize as a former corporate slave. This curly-sideburns man might be surprisingly skilled.

"Farewell, Father. I look forward to when we're able to play together."

My lady calls to Papa as the carriage moves off.

"Master, just leave the young lady to me!"

"Remember, Gandolf, I don't care if you're being entertained. No drinking."

All the ladies call out to Papa from their carriages in turn as he walks away.

The image of Papa nodding gets smaller and smaller until I can no longer see him.

Lady Mary is smiling, but she still looks a little lonely.

I make sure to nuzzle her face lots and lots.

† † †

We arrive at an inn, and Lady Mary and the others leave their belongings with the front desk. After a quick break in our rooms, we decide to head out and explore the city.

I'm going, too, of course.

I'm happy to laze around a fancy hotel, but I can do that at the mansion anytime.

"Please wait just a moment while I call the driver, my lady."

"Wait, Miranda."

Lady Mary calls out to Miranda before she can summon the carriage.

"It's not often we're in the Royal Capital. I was hoping we could explore on foot."

"But…"

Miranda looks over to Hecate. She's probably worried about Lady Mary's health.

I don't think they need to be so overly protective of her. My lady and I normally go for walks around the mansion, and her illness seems cured, thanks to the medicine Hecate made from the wyrmnil.

"Let's see."

The witch, sprawled out on the luxurious lobby sofa, audaciously recrosses her legs.

Tch, I didn't even manage to catch a glimpse.

"As your physician, I see no reason to limit yourself."

She flashes me a look.

"You will have your bodyguard with you. I don't think there should be any problem with going downtown."

Yeah, but please don't expect me to fight or anything. Remember, I'm just a good-for-nothing pup.

"Yes! Please leave it to me! I, Zenobia, shall protect everyone here should the need arise!"

She stands at attention with her fist against her left chest in salute.

Wow, she actually looks like a knight we can depend on. It's a shame no one knows how useless she really is.

The real problem is that when Hecate said "bodyguard," she wasn't talking about Zenobia!

"Yippee! Then let's go! Come on, Doctor, time to get up!"

Oomph. My lady huffs through her nose as she pulls on Hecate's hand.

"Yes, yes. Is there anywhere in particular you'd like to go?"

"Not at all. I just want to walk around with everyone."

"Arwf, arwf! *(I know! I know! We should walk around and try different foods! Let's get something from a food stall that's deep-fried and bad for your body!)*"

"Mewl. *(Oooh, that sounds good.)*"

"I could do with an ice-cold beer."

Slobber. Witch, cat, and dog all stand there drooling. Len is sleeping peacefully, as always. If she was hungry, she'd be awake, too.

"Let's go, everyone!"

And so, we head out.

My lady leads the way as we walk through the Royal Capital.

The Royal Capital has four layers of walls, with different residential districts between each one and the castle in the center. This arrangement is probably another monster deterrent.

The royal family lives in the castle. Just outside the walls surrounding the castle is uptown, where the nobles and aristocrats live. Then there's midtown and downtown, with walls between them. It seems the residential areas are separated by wealth and class.

Of course, the uptown area we're exploring is the safest, and it has fancy buildings lining the streets.

So many of the pedestrians are wearing expensive-looking clothes. With guards patrolling the streets and maintaining public order, everything seems calm and safe.

Zenobia's on edge, looking around like a hawk, but there isn't a hint of danger.

If anything, everyone's giving us suspicious looks.

"Arww. *(Sorry, I lied.)*"

They're giving *me* suspicious looks. I can hear the murmurs of gossip.

My wolf ears are sharp. My lady and the others can't seem to hear them, but their voices reach me loud and clear.

"*What is that giant creature...?!*"

"*A wolf...?! No, it's much bigger than a wolf...!*"

"*Just look at its massive fangs and scary eyes. What a strange pattern on its body. It's not a monster, is it...?*"

"*Why aren't the imperial guards saying anything? It doesn't have anything to do with Morgan's daughter, does it? We should steer clear of it if that's the case...*"

They're murmuring. They're murmuring a lot.

Ugh, I hate that I can hear them whispering about me. This sucks.

The only way to heal this broken heart is to eat street food till I drop.

"Woof, woof! *(Let's buy all the food! All of it! It's all Papa's money anyway!)*"

"Wow, this looks so good!"

I don't even have to say anything before my lady rushes over to a food stand and orders something. I blink in surprise.

We drink a cold, finely blended drink made from crushed whole strawberries. The sweet and tart fruity flavor is amazing.

"Arwf? *(This is just a smoothie, isn't it?)*"

The young man working the stand is crushing the berries so small that when the drink is finally served, it's unmistakably a smoothie.

"Even the food stands in the bazaar of uptown are incredibly high quality. The ingredients are so fresh. They've got price tags to match, though..."

"We cannot have you consuming strange foods, my lady. This level of quality is the lowest I will allow."

Maid Miranda's standards are pretty high. Anything that doesn't have a license from the guild is vetoed. She also goes through tasting everything for poison herself before finally giving it to Lady Mary.

Even now, she's testing the food stand's offerings, taking a slurp from the thick straw.

...Miranda, you're not just using the "checking for poison" thing as an excuse to pig out, are you?

"What, do you want some, too? ...I'm not really a fan of sweet things. You can have the rest of mine."

Zenobia mistakes me staring up at Miranda for jealousy and offers me her cup.

"Arwf? *(Huh? Really?)*"

What's this? Is Zenobia showing her cute side? Is it really okay for me to have this?

"D-don't misunderstand. Scraps are good enough for the likes of you."

Ahhh, that's more like it. Gotta have the *tsun* with the *dere*, after all.

"Arwf! *(Whoa, this is so good! Is this yogurt mixed with apples?)*"

The honey dribbled on top adds a lot of sweetness, but the tartness of yogurt cuts through, making it very palatable.

"Mew! Mew! *(Mistress! I want some, too! Let me try some!)*"

Nahura, riding on Hecate's shoulder, begs by swatting at her with a paw.

"Oh, you want some?"

"Mew! *(Yes please!)*"

"Reeeally?"

Pretending to play dumb, Hecate holds out the cup so it's just out of reach of Nahura's tongue.

"M-mrow! *(M-Mistress! You're so meeeeaaaan!)*"

Those two are always doing stuff like this.

Once she's teased her enough, Hecate lets Nahura have the rest.

The streets of the Royal Capital are lively, but everything is so orderly that there isn't a single piece of trash anywhere.

Once we finish our drinks, someone whom I assume is a cleaner comes over and takes our cups like it's no big deal. If someone collects the trash before you can throw it away yourself, then of course there won't be any litter on the ground. Having a job for even the smallest things is wonderful.

The cleaner quickly runs away the moment they spot me, though. I'm hurt.

You don't need to be so afraid of me. I may be a little big for my age, but I'm still just a two-month-old puppy!

"Oh! Look at this place, Routa!"

Lady Mary points at a store.

"Arwf? *(Hmm? I feel like I've seen this place before. Or maybe not?)*"

There's a banner with a paw print painted on it outside the shop. I can see people on the street looking in and fussing over the kittens and puppies in the front window.

"Arwf! *(Oh, I know!)*"

This is the pet shop I was reborn in!

Ah, the nostalgic place of my birth, though I don't really feel nostalgic for it. My very first memory in this world is of my lady picking me up, after all.

"We met for the very first time here. It wasn't that long ago, but it still feels a little nostalgic, right, Routa?"

"Woof. *(Yeah. I'm really glad you were the one that bought me, Lady Mary.)*"

I've had a few issues here and there, but I have no complaints about my day-to-day life. I am over the moon with the pet life I've always dreamed of.

"Arwf! *(Wait, I just remembered!)*"

The collar! A collar! This is a pet shop, right? Then it should have collars!

"Arwf! Arwf! *(My lady! Let's go in! Let's go in!)*"

I run over to the shop and bat at the door with my forepaw.

"What's wrong, Routa? Do you want to go in?"

She tilts her head as she opens the door.

"Awrooo! *(Excuse me! I'd like a collar, please!)*"

"Yes, welcome! What kind of pet are you loo…king…for…?"

My eyes meet the shop assistant's as he comes to greet his latest customers.

Oh, wait, I recognize those round glasses. I'm sure this is the same person who sold me to Papa Gandolf.

"Woof! Woof! *(Shopkeep! I would like your finest collar!)*"

Who cares how much it costs? Papa's loaded!

"E-eeeeeeeek! A-a monster?!"

"Woof! Woof! *(Oh no, not you, too! I'm not a monster! I'm barking, aren't I? I'm clearly a dog!)*"

"Woof! Woof!" *(See?)* "Woof! Woof! Woof!"

"Ahhhhhhhhhhh! S-someone save meeeeeee!"

"We can't get in if you're standing there, Routa."

While I'm at a loss for what to do with the shopkeeper, who's collapsed while trying to run away, my lady shoves at my butt from behind.

Oh, excuse me.

She's powerless to move my rear, which won't budge even slightly, so I move it out of her way.

"Hello, mister."

"Uhhh...huh? O-oh, you're......"

The frantic shopkeeper finally calms down when he sees my lady.

Her smile has the power to make anyone feel calm.

"You're that customer who bought the puppy that wasn't on my list! Which means this giant white creature is...?!"

"Yes. He's that puppy. He's all grown up."

The shopkeeper stares at my lady after she innocently replies, and a crack appears in his glasses.

"Wh-wh-what have I done...?! I am so sor—"

Uh-oh. The manager's gonna blow my cover.

Hold it right there, mister. I can't have that. Not at all!

"Arwf! Arwf! *(Hey, shopkeep! Over here! Look over here!)*"

I desperately try to catch his attention, cutting off his apology midsentence, his mouth hanging open.

"Arwf, arwf! *(Listen. You're about to tell her what I really am. If you tell her I'm a monster, then you're going to be in trouble, too, for selling me, right?)*"

"Mmmm...!"

I fix him with a death glare and try my best to convey the meaning behind it.

"Arwf, arwf! *(A pet shop that sells monsters will definitely go bankrupt! At the very least, your sales will plummet! There isn't an adult alive who wouldn't pretend they didn't see anything!)*"

"Mmmm......!"

"Woof! Woof! *(Use your common sense! A businessman must think of his profits! Where's your commercial spirit?!)*"

I'm being really hard on him, but I also can't have him spilling the beans.

If anyone else finds out what I really am, I'll be in big trouble, and so will you. There's really only one solution.

"Woof! *(Protect the shop! Which means protecting me!)*"

Come on! Understand what I'm saying!

"Mmmmmm......!"

His face wrinkles up, and his head droops in thought. Then he finally looks up again.

"Wh-wh-wha—?"

"Wha...?"

Lady Mary tilts her head in confusion as the manager puts on his best salesman smile.

"Wh-what a cute dog he's grown into. I can tell you're taking good care of him! It's fantastic!"

Nice one, manager. To survive in these difficult times, it's necessary to play the long game. That's why you should do your best to have my back. Make sure no more information slips, okay?

"Thank you very much. Isn't that great, Routa? He called you cute."

"Arwf, arwf. *(Aw, you're making me blush. Shall I wink? I think I'll wink.* Wink-☆ Wink-☆*)*"

"Urgh..."

Hey.

"So anyway, how can I help you today?"

His will is stronger now that he's mentally prepared himself. He's done a complete reboot, and now he's back in shopkeeper mode.

"Oh, was there something you wanted, Routa?"

My lady looks at me, and I remember why I wanted to come here in the first place.

That's right, my true goal. I came in here to get a collar.

"Arwf? *(Where are they?)*"

I scan the store.

Sure, I could talk to the puppies and kittens in their cages, but I don't have any reason to. The only one my lady should fuss over is me.

"Woof! *(There!)*"

I spot them on a wall covered in pet equipment like cat toys and pet bowls.

"Arww, arww! *(My lady! This! Buy this!)*"

I carry over an extremely glossy enameled red-leather collar in my mouth.

When you think of a white dog, you think red collar. It's a given.

"You want a collar? Won't it be hard to breathe?"

"Arwf! *(Not at all—it'll be fine. If anything, I want to be bound to you.)*"

It'll just make me more dependent, right? Bring it on, my lady.

"Very well, then. Miranda?"

"Yes, miss."

Miranda, who was waiting patiently behind us, suddenly appears, handing money over to the manager.

"Bark! Bark! *(Hurry up! Hurry up! Put it on! Put it on!)*"

"Whoa, calm down, Routa."

I leap up and down on my front paws, causing the shop to shake. Whoops, I should hold back.

"Stay still, okay?"

Yes! The day I get irrefutable proof that I'm the pet of my beloved master has arrived at last…! With this, no one can ever call me Fenrir again…!

"Um, Routa…"

"Arwf? *(Huh? What's wrong?)*"

"The collar won't go on…"

"Arwf…! *(N-no way! I'm sure I picked up the largest one…!)*"

"Gngh!"

Lady Mary tries as hard as she can to latch the collar, but my neck's so thick that it won't even reach halfway.

Damn. Why does my massive body have to get in the way at a time like this?!

"Sir, might you have a slightly larger size?"

Miranda does the smart thing and asks the shopkeeper.

"E-er, I do have something, but…"

"Woof! Woof! *(Huh? You do?! You should have it out if you do! Gimme! Gimme! Give it here!)*"

"Money is no object. We'll take it."

Miranda bows politely.

"Well, it is taking up some room in the storage…"

With that, the shopkeeper brings out a collar from the back of the store that looks like it definitely won't be too small.

It's a perfect fit, but—

"—Thank you for your patronage! Please come again!"

He has a huge grin on his face from selling an item that was just gathering dust in storage. He bows deeply as we leave the store.

"Arwf… (Sigh… *Hey, what are you up to, Zenobia?)*"

"S-soooo cuuuute… Huh?!"

The moment I think about how Zenobia has been missing this whole time, I see her squatting down by the back of the glass case fawning over the puppies.

"A-ahem."

The moment she spots me, she clears her throat and collects herself.

"You better not have caused any problems for the young lady. What did you even get—?"

She points at my neck.

"…What is that?"

"…Arwf. *(…It's a collar.)*"

But it's a cow collar!

Clang-a-lang.

A pastoral bell chime matches my steps.

"Arwww… *(It's somewhat different from what I had hoped for…)*"

With this, I feel less like a pet and more like cattle.

I wanted to become a pampered pooch, not livestock.

I'm rather frustrated by the great quality of this collar. The leather is well tanned and fits nicely. It's actually really comfortable, damn it.

"Arwf... *(Well, the sound of this stupid bell might help trick people. I guess I'll use it...)*"

"Pfft. So all you wanted was a collar."

"Arwf! *(What's wrong with that? There's nothing wrong with a domesticated pup wanting a collar!)*"

"Yeeees. But that's a cow collar."

"Arwf. *(*Sniff. *I just wanted a regular collar.)*"

"You really are strange, Routa... Hmm, what shall we do?"

Hecate notices my depression and places her fingertip on her lip, in thought.

"Routa! That shop has a fantastic smell!"

I immediately forget everything at the sound of my lady's voice.

"Bark! Bark! *(Oh, you're right! I'll go anywhere you lead, my lady!)*"

Lady Mary is my number one priority. I find the spot she's slipped away to, and we descend upon a new food stand.

"Haruff, haruff! *(These hash browns are so good! I looove fried food like that. The high-class food of the mansion can't be beat, but sometimes I've just gotta have junk food like this.)*"

It might be because of the thick layer of flour, but the outside of the hash browns is nice and crunchy while the inside is soft, similar to deep-fried bread. It's delicious.

I devour the golden-brown hash browns one after the other, sparing no concern for the uncivilized noises coming from my mouth.

"Mewl! *(Ah, ish hot! Sho hot!)*"

"You have such a sensitive tongue, Nahura."

"Mew, mewl! *(Please, Mistress, don't say that as you shove more of those hot things into my mouth!)*"

Hmm, business as usual.

"Mmm, mmm... These are—"

"—delicious, yes, but I'm worried that all this fried food will make me fat..."

Zenobia is happily munching away on a hash brown while Miranda worries about her calorie intake.

Both of them are in amazing shape, so I don't think they have anything to worry about. Then again, I'm not exactly an expert on the complexities of women. I just leave them to it.

"I'm so glad we decided to walk around all these food stands, Routa."

"Woof! Woof! *(It's the best! What's next on the menu? I smell something good over there!)*"

I wag my tail in response to my smiling lady.

Then we wander around town, shopping and buying even more food.

Just as we're getting quite stuffed, and the conversation shifts to where we should go next, Hecate stops right in front of a building.

"There's something I need to do. Can you please wait here for a bit?"

"Yes, of course."

It's quite a spectacular building, built in a way that makes the appearance a lot more menacing than the shops.

The sign up on the building has been engraved with the image of a sword wreathed in flames.

The structure is concealed by sturdy walls and fences that you wouldn't be able to break through easily, with two guards standing outside the double iron doors.

"Wait, this is..."

Do you know this place, Zenobia?! ......Zenobia? Hello? Why are you hiding behind me?

Zenobia crouching down behind me, trying to look as small as possible, is pretty cute, but what in the world is this store?

"Halt."

"This is the headquarters of the Adventurers Guild. What business do you have here? If you are an adventurer, please present your adventurer's license."

The guards ask politely because this is the uptown district, after all, but their demeanor is still quite intimidating.

Hecate doesn't shy away from them and instead beams a charming smile.

"Is the guild leader in? I would like a word with her."

"Do you have an appointment? If not, you will need a letter of recommendation from another branch."

"Really? I don't have anything like that… Could I ask for a teeny-tiny favor? Just tell her the witch of Feltbelk Forest is here to see her."

The guards look at each other, then tell her to wait a moment while one goes inside.

I had imagined the Adventurers Guild to be a rough place, but it seems to be a surprisingly upscale establishment where they'll happily refuse you at the door.

Oh yeah, Zenobia's an ex-adventurer. I wonder if she's hiding behind me because she doesn't want to meet any old acquaintances of hers.

Her situation can't be like James's where she made some kind of grave mistake, could it…?

…Yeah, it's definitely something like that. My gut tells me so. I mean, it's Zenobia.

Less than a minute after the guard disappears inside, we hear frantic footsteps.

Wham. The door flies open.

"Hecate! You! Pick now of all times to brazenly wander back…!"

A mature office-lady-looking woman with a blouse and pencil skirt comes flying out of the building with fire in her eyes. She's pretty sexy, honestly. Her glasses have a thin chain on them, and there's a mole under one of her eyes. A real beauty.

"Do you have any idea how crazy things have been since you vanished?! It's been a hundred years since I've heard from you! What have you been doing?!

A hundred years? That's an insanely long time.

Now that I look a little closer, this woman has long ears and silver hair just like Hecate.

I guess, like Hecate, she doesn't look her age, but maybe it's because they're members of the same race?

"I see you haven't changed, Emerada. Still as angry as ever. Have you gained even more wrinkles?"

"Y-you…! How do you still look so young when you're so much older than me…?!"

"Because I'm a witch?"

"Some witch you are! Honestly… So? Why in the world are you here? I'm busy trying to deal with some kind of powerful magical disaster that happened in the northeast."

She puts her hand on her hip and sighs. Yep, still sexy.

I wouldn't mind getting told off by a boss like her. I wanna be abused by section chief Emerada's heels.

Just kidding. I've had enough of corporate life.

"Do you know about it? We detected abnormal levels of magical energy near the sacred mountain just north of the border of the Faulks estate. It was so strong that we were able to observe it from here."

Huh? Did she just say "Faulks"? Does that have something to do with us?

"I haven't seen powerful magic like that since the Great Demon Lord War one thousand years ago. The royal palace is making a big fuss, saying it's an omen of the Demon Lord's revival. They demanded the guild conduct an immediate investigation.

"Yes, about that. Would you mind calling off the investigation?"

"Wh-what?! Why…? Wait. Did you have something to do with that?!"

"How rude. It wasn't me at all."

Huh? Why did she just look at me? Hecate, please.

"It wasn't? This wouldn't be the first time you've been reckless."

I suppose it's because they're old acquaintances that section chief Emerada's tone is getting more and more frank.

"That's why I'm wondering if you could hold off the investigation. Or perhaps just postpone it for a little bit?"

"Hmph, you're too late! I sent out able-bodied adventurers to the area a while ago!"

Section chief Emerada puffs out her chest with pride, causing her assets above to jiggle. Now that's what I'm talkin' about! Keep it up, section chief Emerada!

No, wait, she's not a section chief; she's the guild leader. But for some reason, she emits this aura that makes me want to call her Chief. Maybe it's her tired face and head-to-toe pessimism.

"I made a specialist team of A-Rank scouts. It was a pressing matter, so they left right away. They should arrive in less than two weeks."

"Oh my, really? That's a little sooner than I had planned."

"'Planned'? What are you talking about?"

"Oh, just talking to myself."

"...So you *do* know something?"

"Tee-hee, I wonder."

The chief raises her eyebrows suspiciously, and Hecate smiles at her.

"Ugh, honestly! It's been forever, but you still get on my nerves! Come here! I'm taking the rest of the day off! You're telling me everything over a drink!"

"So forward!"

Hecate is dragged by the arm toward the door.

"My apologies, everyone, but it looks like this is where we part ways."

"Mrow. *(Then I, too, shall partake in the merriment. Hee-hee-hee. Alcohol—)*"

"Arwf! *(Huh? No fair!)*"

I wanna drink, too. Damn that Nahura. I'm going to bat her around like a toy when she gets back.

"See you tomorrow."

Hecate waves back to us by the gate before heading inside with the chief.

"That's a shame, but having friends is important."

My lady looks a little sad.

"Woof! Woof! *(Lady Mary! Cheer up! You've still got me!)*"

"Ha-ha, what's wrong, Routa?"

She ruffles my head.

Tch. I wanted to cheer you up, but now you're comforting me. It's hard not to feel frustrated.

"The sun's starting to set. Why don't we head back to the inn for today?"

"Arwf! *(Yeah! Let's leave the terrible day-drinking adults behind and laze around the fancy hotel.)*"

Speaking of the hotel, I'm really looking forward to dinner tonight.

I wonder what's on the menu, heh-heh-heh.

† † †

"Oh, Routa, look over there. Over by that church wall."

We're walking back when my lady suddenly stops and points toward a church.

"Arwf? *(Hmm? There's something over there.)*"

It's a stone statue of a young man holding a sword aloft.

I don't know if the credit lies with the craftsman's impressive skills, but even though the statue's made of stone, it looks like his cloak is actually waving in the wind.

The impressive pose he strikes with his sword held high practically screams "hero."

"He's the reason I named you Routa."

"Arwf. *(Oh. Well, my name was actually Routa to begin with.)*"

"He's the hero Routa who defeated the evil Demon Lord and brought peace to the world one thousand years ago!"

"Arw. *(Hmm, well, we might both be named Routa, but I guess the similarities end there.)*"

It's a little annoying how handsome that statue is. Maybe I should pee on it.

Just as I get jealous of the stone statue my lady admires so much, I hear a crowd of voices from the other direction.

"Run for it, everyone! The monster girl is coming!"

"Hurry, or you'll be dead meat!"

"People with strange pets should hide! Or they'll be taken away!"

A mixture of people, men and women, old and young, come running toward us in a huge group.

"Arwf? *(What's going on?)*"

It looks like they're running from something.

Wait. Hold it, hold it. Won't it be dangerous if they keep running this way? They're on a collision course with us!

This really is dangerous! Not good! They're going to crash into us! Right into us!

"Arwf! *(Whoa, whoa, whoa! Excuse me, my lady!)*"

"H-huh? Routa?"

Just before we're about to be swallowed by the throng of people, I scoop my lady up from below. Her light body rests on my back, and I jump high into the air.

I leap over the wave of people and land on the edge of the road with Lady Mary safely on my back.

"Huh? What?"

My lady looks around puzzled, not knowing what just happened.

I should have acted like a normal pet, but with such a narrow road, there wasn't anywhere else to go. I had no choice.

"Woof, woof! *(Zenobia! Miranda! Are you all right?)*"

I'm pretty sure Zenobia should have been able to react, but I can't see them anywhere.

"My lady! Are you all right?!"

Zenobia calls over from the other side of the wave of people. Looks like they were able to get out on that side.

"I'm fine! Routa saved me! You're not hurt at all, are you?"

"N-no, Ms. Zenobia was able to protect me!"

Nice one, Zenobia. Looks like she was able to save Miranda, too.

But there's no end to this crowd. It's so packed in front of us that I can't take a single step into the flow of people.

"...Hey, you guys are in the way! Move!"

"Ms. Zenobia, please refrain from anything that will make you stand out or appear to be of a higher station than them... We're in the uptown district, so there's a chance there is a noble among them. If you do anything to cause issues for the family, then..."

"Grr, but at this rate, we won't be able to regroup with the young lady...!"

I can hear Miranda pacifying Zenobia, who's unable to clear the wall of people.

Hmm, I wonder if I should jump over there with Lady Mary on my back.

"We'll be fine. Routa's with me, so let's split up and meet back at the inn!"

Well, leave it to Lady Mary to be the one worrying about them.

"Tch, but... No, this isn't a safe place to stop, either... Very well. We'll head over there right away!"

"We'll be fine; don't worry about us!"

"Routa! You better protect her!"

"Woof! *(You got it!)*"

You shouldn't expect so much from a pet, but I can at least help my lady run away.

We split up from Zenobia and Miranda and head in a different direction.

Slipping down a narrow road to get away from the crowd of people, we eventually come out on a nearby street.

"Phew. That was a surprise. I wonder what that was all about."

"Arwf. *(No idea. I feel like someone said something about a monster?)*"

A monster isn't going to jump out at us, is it?

The royal guards need to get their act together. It's their job to protect the people of the city.

Oh wait, I suppose I'm a potential target for elimination. Never mind! Please keep working in moderation.

"It's so quiet."

"Arwf, arwf. *(Yeah.)*"

It might be because it's late afternoon, or because of all the noise just now, but there doesn't seem to be anyone populating the dimly lit streets.

I'm at least grateful the whispering of the townsfolk has stopped.

"Woof, woof. *(Oh, Lady Mary. Not that way, I'm pretty sure this is the right street.)*"

I'm not Zenobia, so I actually have a good sense of direction.

"This way? Oh, Routa, you're so smart."

"Arwf. *(Heh-heh-heh, Zenobia's not like me, though, not at all.)*"

Miranda's probably being dragged all over the place by Zenobia right now.

She has no sense of direction, but she's so sure of herself that she just marches on ahead.

"Hee-hee, the two of us haven't been on a walk alone together since that time."

"Arwf? *(Which time?)*"

Oh, I know. The time we snuck out of the mansion and went to play by the lake.

We walked along the road we always take in the carriage, but Lady Mary ended up getting tired and falling asleep.

That was the time I found out I was less of a wolf and more of a monster. I noticed goblins deep in the forest, so I went to go scare them, but for some reason, I shot a beam from my mouth…

It wasn't that long ago, but it feels like it's been ages since that happened.

"Hey, Routa, back then, what really—?"

She stops.

"Arwf? *(What's wrong, my lady? Do you need another nap?)*"

"………No, it's nothing. Let's be together forever."

With that, she wraps her arms around my neck and squeezes me tight.

"Woof! Woof! *(Of course! I swear that I'll be yours for the rest of my life!)*"

I can feel her gentle warmth through my fur, when suddenly, there's a shadow.

"……Arwf? *(…Hmm? What the—?)*"

I look up to see—

"Ohhh-ho-ho-ho! What a peculiar dog you have there, commoner!"

—a stereotypical snobby young lady with a cliché high-pitched laugh.

03 A Forced Invitation! ...Or So I Thought, but It Turned into a Rampage!

"Arwf…? *(Wait, 'ohhh-ho-ho-ho'?…Seriously?)*"

I didn't think people who laughed like that actually existed. She even puts the back of her hand up to her mouth perfectly.

She has bright-red gloves and a bright-red dress. Her eyes scream "Jackpot!" and she smiles like she's plotting something.

And then there's the thing that ties it all together: her magnificent curls. They're a deep golden color, like a lion's mane. They're done up in the legendary "twin drills" hairstyle and look like they could dig straight into the ground.

"Woof, woof. *(Hey, we can see your panties. You all right with that, Drills?)*"

She's wearing a beautiful dress, but standing so high above us means that when the wind blows, we can see *everything.*

"Arwf, arwf. *(Oh man, it's worse when I can't actually let her know. So rough on me. So she's wearing black ones, huh? I mean, this is just the worst.)*"

Lady Mary still has no idea what's going on as she stares at the unexpected intruder.

I don't know if Drills notices my lady's confusion, but she makes a decisive pose.

"I am Elizabeth! Elizabeth Morgan!"

Hearing her introduction, Lady Mary snaps out of it and replies.

"I-it's a pleasure to make your acquaintance. My name is Meariya Vo—"

"I do not care for the names of commoners!"

"Huuuh?! R-really?!"

How rude! That's completely ridiculous.

"I mean, ugh, just *look* at yourself!"

"Ohhh-ho-ho-ho!" She sways as she laughs in a high-pitched voice.

Wait, she's calling my lady a commoner, but Lady Mary is the daughter of an aristocrat. She's the only daughter of multimillionaire Marquis Gandolf Von Faulks.

Socially speaking, she's nowhere near commoner. Her family name even has *Von* in it.

And I feel like I've heard the name Morgan before. It makes me think of that Morgan guy with the curly sideburns.

Is it okay for her to act like this? Doesn't she know what'll happen?

"I don't care about you! What I *am* interested in is that dog! That glossy fur, those eyes, that size! It's simply spectacular!"

"Th-thank you very much. Hee-hee-hee. She praised you, Routa."

I'm not exactly happy about being praised by an excavation drill, but Lady Mary's smile is super-cute, so I'll let it slide.

It's no problem at all. Praise me all you want.

"The more I look, the more beautiful he becomes. Which is why I had a thought. Such a marvelous creature should belong not with a commoner, but with me!"

"......Arwf? *(......Hmm? What the hell did she just say?)*"

If we're talking about pets, the only master for me is Lady Mary and no one else.

"Now then, hand him over to me! I shall grant you anything you desire! It's an offer you can't refuse!"

"Woof. *(I refuse.)*"

"I refuse."

We respectfully refuse.

It's a spectacular synchronicity between master and pet.

"Wh-what did you say?!"

"I said I refuse. Routa is an important member of the family."

Lady Mary replies with a massive grin.

"Arwf! Arwf! *(Yeah! Yeah! First of all, she has a private airship and an incredible chef! Beautiful maids as well—it's great!)*"

But more importantly, I have no interest in a household without Lady Mary!

"Ho-ho-ho........... Ohhh-ho-ho-ho! You sure have guts for a commoner!"

Your smile's frozen, Drills.

"Very well! What do you think of this?! Christina! Come give this little girl a scare!"

"Who's Christina?"...is what I'd like to ask, but before I can, I hear the rustling of the scaffolding beneath her.

"A-arwf...... *(Wh-whoooaaa...!)*"

I was wondering what she was standing on to be in such a high place, but it turns out to be a giant creature. Perhaps it's because the sun is setting and creating a backlight that I didn't notice sooner. Standing there on two legs is a reptile— No, wait, maybe I should call it a dragon?

She slowly lowers her front legs to the ground and then sluggishly turns to face us.

Her thick scales and the way she moves on her four limbs makes her look more like an alligator.

Ohhh, so that wave of people that ran into us was running away from *this*.

"Arwf...! *(Whoa, she's huuuuge...!)*"

Drills has a pretty impressive pet.

"GRRRR..."

Following her master's orders, the dragon growls at us.

Ha-ha-ha, goodness me. You're quite intense. I daresay I may have voided my bladder just a tad.

"Arwf... *(What should I do? The idea of actually wetting myself in front of Lady Mary is unbearable...)*"

I stare into the vertical pupils of the dragon's reptilian eyes…… and she stops her intimidating gestures.

"Arwf? *(Huh? What?)*"

The reptile stares at my tense face as I try my best not to pee, and for some reason, she starts to tremble.

"Arwf, arwf? *(Whoa, what's wrong? Do you have a chronic illness or something?)*"

Worried, I take a step forward, and the dragon takes a step back in fear.

"Squee… *(It's most likely because inferior magical creatures are stricken with fear when my darling glares at them.)*"

It looks like the dragon who made her home in my fur has finally woken up.

Len peeks her face out of my mane and yawns.

"Squee. *(When you glared at me and claimed your domain, I was so scared, my scales stood on end, but my heart was also set aflame.)*"

Yeah, no, don't make it sound like a proposal.

Wait, is she talking about the first time we met, when I peed everywhere? When I was so scared of her that I completely wet myself? How do you spin that memory into something positive?

"What's wrong, Christina?! Why are you afraid?!"

"G-grrrr…"

Drills is bewildered by her dragon (who doesn't look like a "Christina" at all) retreating in fear.

"Now go! And give them a terrifying roar!"

She stamps her high-heeled foot on the dragon's head.

Um, you shouldn't do that on such an unstable surface…

"Roar! Roar, I say! —Ahhh!"

Just as I thought, she loses her balance and falls off.

"Ahhhhhhhhhhh?!"

"Woof, woof. *(Yeah, yeah, I'm comin'… Aaand gotcha!)*"

I move to where she's about to fall and catch her on my back. She plunges into my fur, slips off my rear, and plops onto the ground.

"Arwf. *(Hmph, you'd better be grateful to my fluff.)*"

"Wh-what just happened? What was that…?!"

The girl who just fell on her butt looks around in shock before she starts to cry.

So she's haughty yet weak willed; I don't *not* like it. Maybe I should lick her?

"Squee? *(So what's this all about?)*"

Len just woke up, so of course she has no clue. I give her a quick rundown of what's happened so far.

"Arwf. *(To put it simply, you missed out on street food.)*"

That street food was so good. The best junk food I've had in a while.

"Squeak! *(N-no fair! Why didn't you wake me?! I was hungry, too!)*"

"Arwf… *(Really, all you ever do is eat and sleep…)*"

Damn, Len's living the ideal NEET life. I might actually respect her a little.

"Squeak, squeak. *(What was that? I'll have you know I perform an important service whispering sweet nothings into your ear each day.)*"

Yeah, I really don't need that.

"Um, are you all right?"

Lady Mary holds out a handkerchief to Drills, who's still crying.

"U-uwaah, thank you…… This handkerchief is of surprisingly high quality."

She sniffles, takes a deep breath, then stands up.

"Ohhh-ho-ho-ho! You saved me! You may be a commoner, but I am in your debt! I must thank you!"

That is a quick recovery.

"Let us be off! I am inviting you to my home! Then you will see once and for all who that dog is best suited for!"

Oh, she hasn't given up.

Then again, if she sees me only as a dog, she might be even more clueless than I thought.

"Bark, bark? *(Come on, Lady Mary. Can't we just we leave her and head back?)*"

I try to call out to my lady, but she's not listening. Her cheeks are completely flushed.

"I've never...been invited to a friend's house before!"

"S-s-s-since when are we friends?! Don't get the wrong idea!"

Drills is totally flustered by how happy my lady is. She tries to hide her face quickly, but it's easy to tell that she's so embarrassed, even her ears are red.

I guess she doesn't have any friends.

My lady is the same. I feel like these two could actually get along surprisingly well.

"G-grrrr..."

Perhaps it's because she hasn't received an order in a while or because she just dropped her mistress, but the dragon lets out an uneasy growl.

"What are you doing, Christina? I, your mistress Elizabeth, am not so narrow-minded that I would scold you just for one or two mistakes."

"Grrrr...!"

She whips her tail happily and lowers her head so Drills can climb up.

"Let's go, Routa."

"Arww. *(Aw... But Miranda and Zenobia are waiting. Shouldn't we get back as soon as possible?)*"

"We're not going back right now."

"Arww? *(Really...?)*"

Sigh. Here we go again... Lady Mary can be surprisingly stubborn.

Meanwhile, in the downtown area of the Royal Capital...

"Tch, where are we...?! Why can't we find the inn...?!"

Zenobia groans, sweat pouring down her brow.

"Why? Because this is *downtown*! Our inn is *uptown*!"

Miranda, who has been holding it in as she walks behind Zenobia, finally snaps.

"What did you say?! This isn't uptown?!"

"Are you serious?! Please pull yourself together, Zenobia! For mercy's sake, please let me lead the way!"

"No! I shall not allow it! I must lead the way so that nothing happens to you in such a dangerous place!"

"But it was you who led us to such a dangerous place to begin with! …Oh, I do hope the young lady is safe…!"

Miranda clasps her hands together and prays to the goddess, as Zenobia looks left and right, checking a crossroad.

"Damn it! I know the inn is somewhere north! All right then, this way!"

"That way leads south! Ms. Zenobia, please at least let me decide which direction we go!"

"No! An amateur's decision-making could be perilous in a place such as this! I shall lead the way! You'll be safe with me! I am a combat specialist, after all!"

"But I already said that it was *you* who led us to such a dangerous area!"

Her desperate pleas never reach the airheaded knight.

Who knows when the two of them will ever reach the inn.

† † †

"Here we are!"

Drills strikes another pompous pose in front of a magnificent mansion.

We're still in the city, so the garden is fairly small, but the mansion itself is huge.

"Bark… *(This is…quite the place…)*"

The Faulkses' mansion is a calming white with gothic architecture, but this mansion has red walls with a gold roof. It looks like they built the house based on Drills herself.

"Wow. What a wonderful home!"

Whaaaat? Reeeally? I suppose it's not something you see every day, but hearing that is a slap in the face.

"Ha-ha-ha, it is! You have a good eye! Very good! Very good, indeed!"

She puts the palm of her hand up to her mouth, praises Lady Mary, and laughs in a high-pitched voice. She's going to fall off Christina if she gets too cocky again.

""""Welcome back, Lady Elizabeth.""""

A line of servants bow together as they greet Drills.

"I have guests. Prepare tea."

"Yes, ma'am."

After taking her hands and helping her down from the dragon, the servants respectfully clear a path for us.

They open the door, and we enter the mansion, and there we are greeted by decorations so gaudy, they put the outside of the mansion to shame.

"Arwf… *(I'm blind…)*"

"Oh, how pretty!"

"Ohhh-ho-ho-ho! Very good! Very good!"

My lady's compliment sends Drills reeling with ecstasy. As soon as she's asked a question, she answers with genuine excitement.

These two really do look like they'll get along well.

"*Lady Elizabeth brought another strange creature home…*"

My wolf ears are sharp. (Again.)

I can hear the servants talking from one of the corridors.

"*Can't anyone do anything about that strange hobby of hers? It's good that she took the initiative to care for them, but I can't help but worry that they'll escape and attack someone…*"

"*The person who sold them to her kept insisting they would be safe to keep, but I don't know how much we can trust them…*"

"*Every day, she spends all the money she wants. She's just going overboard to distract herself from her loneliness…*"

"*There's also the issue of the master leaving her to her own devices. How long has it been since he last returned to the mansion?*"

"I'm sure it has been at least two or three years. Ever since his wife left him for another lover. Perhaps the master does not wish to return here anymore..."

"It is good that he's working so diligently on his trading business, but I'm sure he doesn't know anything about his daughter's strange hobby..."

Oof. That is a surprisingly heavy conversation.

Seems like Drills is an abandoned child who simply gets money thrown at her.

My lady's mother seems to be out of the picture, too, but I really don't know anything about that. I do know that Papa showers her with love enough for two parents. And even when he's busy, he takes her along on trips like this.

Does this mean Drills doesn't receive any love from her parents...?

"Here we are!"

She guides us through the mansion until we finally reach a door that she throws open.

Was this once a ballroom? The hall's big enough for it.

"A-arwf?! *(Wait, what are those?!)*"

Mountains of cages are piled up inside the hall like a pet shop, with a variety of creatures inside.

"All of these are suitable creatures that have been gathered for me from every region!"

She splays her arms, proudly showcasing the animals.

"Oh, how wonderful! They're all Eliza's friends!"

"'E-Eliza'?! Th-that's rather informal of you... But I'll forgive you! I am a generous person, after all!"

"Thank you very much. You can call me Mary if you like, Eliza."

"Whaaaat?! ...Um......M-Mary...?"

"Yes! What is it, Eliza?"

"...........!"

Drills turns bright red when my lady replies with a smile.

Wow, you're a softy. You're a super-softy, Drills.

"Arwf... *(But something's bugging me. Aren't these all monsters? Every single one of them looks pretty vicious...)*"

The creatures in the cages don't look anything like regular animals. They're super-scary, with less of a roughness and more of a monster-ness about them.

"Squee? *(What are you saying, beloved...? I think you're the most terrifying creature here.)*"

Shut up. Don't say things that chip away at my glass heart. I even try to avoid mirrors so I don't come face-to-face with reality.

"Woof, woof? *(Hey, Len. Me aside, can monsters become friends with humans?)*"

These guys are strangely quiet. Even when my lady and Drills go near them, they don't react at all, staying stock-still in their cages.

If keeping monsters were this normal, then I wouldn't need to worry about hiding what I really am, right? Wouldn't my pet life be secure like this?

"Squee. *(Look at their necks, beloved.)*"

"Arwf? *(Huh?)*"

And that's when I notice that each of them is wearing a magnificent jeweled collar.

"Arwf! *(Wh-what incredible collars! I'm so jealous! Any of you guys wanna trade collars with me?)*"

"Squeak, squeak! *(No, no! Yes, their collars are what I was pointing out, but look closer. They're enchanted. This is no doubt the type of spell that influences the spirit.)*"

"Arwf?! *(What?! They're being brainwashed?!)*"

I know they're monsters, but that's just cruel.

"Squee, squeak. *(That's right. It's unheard of for even low-level monsters to act friendly to humans. The* only *way they would become domesticated like this is if someone used a spell to manipulate them. Although, such a sloppy spell like this wouldn't have any effect on an intelligent dragon like myself!)*"

It's not good to puff yourself up like that.

"Arwf... *(But what about that dragon? She's totally being controlled.)*"

I can see the other dragon outside the window. She looks like she really wants to come inside.

"Squeak, squee, squeak. *(Oh, she's a type of dragon that's a subclass of a subclass. A red dragon with only a thin blood relation. I don't know where they got her, but she must be an idiot if she was captured by the likes of humans. A weak dragon like that could surely be controlled with a spell.)*"

I see. But it doesn't look like this technique was used on that dragon. Elizabeth must have done something with her money power.

Sounds like she was tricked by a bad salesman into buying these creatures. Maybe that's what the servants have been gossiping about.

Wait, so Drills hasn't realized these creatures are monsters? That means she's as clueless as Lady Mary, which would also explain why she hasn't figured out what I really am.

"—And that's how we came to the Royal Capital."

"Oh, so you're staying in that inn? I've heard their upholstery and cuisine are quite fantastic, and the staff are exceptionally skilled. You must have gotten very lucky to be able to stay there. I heard that people from the supreme Faulks Co. had booked out the entire establishment for the next three years."

"Hee-hee-hee, thank you very much."

"I was not praising you at all, honestly. Ha-ha-ha."

Oh wow, when did these two become so close?

They're having a lively chat as they drink the tea the servants brought.

"I see—so you don't live in the Royal Capital."

"My home is a little far from here, but it is most wonderful. I would love to have you over next time, Eliza."

"I—I see. I s-suppose I'll think about it, since you asked."

Looks like Drills has forgotten all about me in the presence of her new friend, Lady Mary.

All's well that ends well. They seem to be having a nice chat. I hope we can go home after they finish their tea.

"Squeak… *(Hmm, this spell…)*"

"Arwf? *(Hmm? What's wrong?)*"

Sounds like there's something on Len's mind.

"Squeak— *(My darling. I have some bad news. This spell is—)*"

Just as Len is about to say something, Drills, who was enjoying her tea up until a moment ago, slams the table.

"No! Why are we sitting around talking?! I brought you here to prove to you that I would be a much better owner for that dog!"

"Wh-whaaaat…?! But we were having so much fun!"

"I—I was t— No! Just listen to me!"

"Very well, then. Let's hear it."

Lady Mary adjusts herself in her seat, resting her arms straight with her hands upon her knees. She looks at Drills with a serious glint in her eye, and Drills clears her throat.

"You saw them, didn't you? All the creatures here. Their fur is glossy, they're healthy, and they can move as much as they like. They're even taken on walks every day."

Well, I guess environmentally it's not bad. There's nothing more delicious than food you can eat lying down.

But the issue is that their eyes are all dead. They're all clouded over.

"Perfect health management is very important for animals! I'm sure you only feed him scraps and don't exercise him at all!"

I guess it's not far from the truth. My meals are always what's left around the mansion, and I spend all day sleeping.

"You cannot maintain an animal's health that way! An owner's responsibility is to give their pets an appropriate amount of exercise and consider the best nutrition for them!"

"Oh, I see."

Lady Mary nods seriously.

Wait a second, my lady. I don't want any of that!

I'm happy with spending every day lazing around and getting stuffed on high-calorie food.

"And the secret to these creatures' health is this! Animal biscuits made by the Morgan Company! It has all the nutrition an animal needs. Everyone loves them!"

With that, she pours a bunch of hard biscuits onto a plate.

"Here, eat up!"

She shoves the plate under my nose.

I guess I'll eat it.

"Arwf. *(It doesn't smell that good, but you shouldn't judge something without trying it.)*"

When I sniff them, they have a weird grassy smell.

"Arwf… *(I'll just start with a bite…)*"

Crunch. Crunch.

"………… *(…………)*"

It's good. There's a pleasant aroma in my nose, and I begin drowning in satisfac— Wha—?! Or not!

"Pleh! Ptooey! *(Gross! What is this?!)*"

I feel all the moisture leave my mouth as my saliva stops and the grassy taste of the biscuit amplifies. They taste terrible, like concentrated weeds.

I don't care how good for you these are; you'd go crazy if you had to eat these all day.

Especially me, because I get to eat food cooked by a crazy-skilled chef every day. I'm always spoiled by his food.

"Arwf! *(Well, my lady wins! I will* never *be your dog!)*"

I show my refusal by nestling right up against Lady Mary.

"Wh-what is the meaning of this…? All my babies love eating these…!"

That's because you've brainwashed them. No one in their right mind would be able to eat these.

"Squee. *(About that. The spell that binds these creatures is going to break soon.)*"

"Arwf? *(Huh?)*"

"Squee. *(There's nothing wrong with the technique used, but to put it simply, the magical power is fading. The spell can't remain active without any power behind it. It's only a matter of time before the brainwashing wears off.)*"

Oh, that's bad.

The moment I think that, I hear something like a *SNAP.*

"Grrrr…"

I turn around to see a broken jeweled collar and a monster with its fangs bared. Its eyes are glowing red. It's clearly enraged.

"Ar-ar-arwoooooo!"

It lets out a wild howl and bites the bars, effortlessly ripping the cage open.

That seems to set off a chain reaction as other monsters start to go wild.

"Wh-what is this?! What's going on?!"

One after the other, the monsters break free and are unleashed upon the room. But it's not quite right to say the brainwashing has worn off. This is unusual. They're just running wild with no clear objective.

"Squee. *(It appears their fighting instinct that was being suppressed has been released all at once.)*"

"Bark? *('It appears'? You sure are relaxed about this… What do we do…?)*"

"Squeak. *(I don't know much about humans. But for anyone to assume they can have their way with monsters is a shortsighted notion and a fool's mistake. They should have known better. You reap what you sow.)*"

No, it seems Drills didn't know anything about the collars. Saying "You reap what you sow" is too harsh.

She took care of them as best she could. It's only turning out this way because of the loneliness she felt without her family around.

Len isn't going to be any help, but no matter what I do, I can't use my powers in front of my lady. Otherwise, she'll find out I'm not a dog.

"Wh-what's wrong, everyone?! I don't understand!"

Drills desperately tries to call out to the monsters, and they all look at her.

""""GRWWWL!""""

"Eek…!"

Was the food really that bad? Their rage is overwhelming. Fangs and claws are bared as if every creature in the room is about to tear her to shreds.

But the one who positions their body in between Elizabeth and the angry horde isn't me, but a scaly behemoth.

"Ch-Christina?!"

The ground dragon Christina has broken through the wall to get inside; her entire body from head to tail wraps around us, acting as a wall of protection.

"Grrr…!"

Christina growls in pain as she's bitten all over.

She should have broken free of the brainwashing, too, but she's protecting Drills.

"Arwf! *(I don't know why you're helping us, but you're all right in my book!)*"

And now, with Lady Mary safely tucked away in the shadow of Christina's giant body, I can comfortably act out of her line of sight.

"Woof! *(Now's my chance!)*"

I leap over Christina's back. The moment I land on the ground, I take a deep breath.

And then—

"Awoooooooooooo!! *(Quiiiiiiiieeeeeeeet!)*"

—my howling voice shakes the mansion, rattling the monsters' eardrums.

It also whips up a wind that cracks the windows and blows over the furniture.

At the same time, my cow collar snaps and goes flying.

Whatever, I don't have time to worry about that. Having that clanging bell around my neck wasn't dignified anyway.

"Arwf. *(Phew… Looks like that calmed things down some.)*"

Trying to howl without firing a beam is harder than I thought.

Luckily, my lady and Drills can't see me. They probably think one of the monsters just howled.

The monsters that were running wild now have their tails tucked between their legs and are lying on the ground. Looks like my voice has brought them back to their senses.

"Woof, woof! *(We don't have much time, so listen up!)*"

I don't know if my intimidation is too effective, but now the monsters are trembling as they hang on my every word.

"Woof, woof! *(You want your freedom, right? Well, here's how you get it. Far to the northeast of here is a massive forest.)*"

It's incredibly far from the Royal Capital, but hopefully, I'll be able to solve the issue of distance.

"Arwf! *(Nahura. Can you hear me? Come to me if you can!)*"

She always appears at just the right time. I'm not sure if that's because she's always watching me, but I know if I call her like this, she's sure to come running.

"Mewl? *(Whaddaya want? I won't be sharin' any of my booze, y'know.)*"

Just as I expected, a portal appears out of thin air, and Nahura comes leaping out of it.

"Hic—"

"Arwf! *(You* reek *of alcohol!)*"

Oh yeah, she was drinking with Hecate.

She's totally hammered. Will this be okay…? I'm a little worried now.

"Woof, woof? *(I'll explain everything later. You see these monsters? Can you teleport them to the northern part of the forest?)*"

"Mew? Mrrow? *(Wha—? Caaan I? I'll have you know I'm an eggshellent familiar! Distance ish no issue at all as long as I have the coordinips.)*"

"Woof, woof? *(You'll get them there safe, right? You won't send them anywhere weird because you're drunk?)*"

"Meow. *(It'll be fiiiine.)*"

I'm a little worried, but she reassures me. Next up are the monsters.

"Woof, woof. *(All right, you guys, I have just one condition.* Never *appear in front of humans. If you can do that, I'll guarantee your freedom.*

The water's clean, and there's lots of fruit. It's a great forest full of nature. I know you'll love it.)"

I feel bad that they'll have to sleep outside, but even as I speak, I can see the light of hope begin to return to their eyes. As far I can tell, these conditions will work in their favor.

"Woof, woof. *(Anyone who agrees should stand in front of this cat.)*"

They line up in front of Nahura on my command.

I knew they all would agree. Looks like none of them have any regrets about leaving this place. I guess it's true that monsters just don't get attached to humans.

"Grrr......"

I stand corrected. A certain dragon seems to want to be the exception. She'll continue protecting Drills like she has up till now.

"Woof, woof. *(All right, when you get to the forest, you should meet some black wolves that look like me. Tell them 'Routa said we can live here'; hopefully, they'll understand. Don't disobey them, even if you don't agree with them.)*"

Because they're super-strong. And professional hunters.

The monsters all nod meekly. I guess they've had enough scary experiences for one lifetime.

"Mewl! *(Space magic activaaate! Reeeady, steeeady, and—teleport!)*"

A white space encircles the monsters, and a moment later, they're gone.

"Meowf. *(Mission compleeeete.)*"

"Arwf. *(Thanks, nice work. That's all I needed. You can go now.)*"

My lady is going to get suspicious if Nahura is here when she wasn't before.

"Mrooow? *(Whaaaat? You call me aaall the way out here, have your way with me, and then send me away when you're dooone? You're such a meeeeaaaaniiiie.)*"

"Arwf. *(Hey, don't cling to me, you drunk. Shoo, shoo.)*"

"Mewl. *(Honestly, you're such a bad dog, Routa.)*"

I shoo her away, and she sighs before stumbling back through another space-magic hole.

All that's left in the hall is deafening silence, with just the wreckage and us.

"What in the world happened...? Where...is everyone? Where did they all go...?"

Christina moves her body out of the way, and Drills just stands there, staring at the empty cages in shock.

"But...why...? Everyone...... Everyone vanished..."

Seeing the lonely girl in the middle of the large empty room is heartbreaking.

"I'm all alone again......"

Forsaken by her parents, shunned by the servants, this girl only had her pets to rely on.

She drops to her knees in tears, and I try to comfort her with a bark.

"Arwf. *(That's not true, Drills.)*"

"You're not alone, Eliza."

My lady hugs her from behind.

"Routa and I are already your friends. Not to mention......"

She gestures to the dragon that protected her master with her own body.

"Grrr..."

She rubs her nose against Drills.

"Christina..."

"Arwf. *(So she's staying here.)*"

"Squee. *(It seems she was never affected by the brainwashing spell to begin with. She serves this child of her own free will. Hmph. 'Tis not every day that a dragon will get close to a human by choice. You should be honored, little girl.)*"

What's this? Len was just saying "You reap what you sow," but now she's acting worried?

This only ended peacefully because of the strong master-pet bond between Christina and Drills.

Still, it will cause problems if anyone sees Len, so I try to hide her in my fur.

"Squeak! *(Gngh. S-stop it. Stop pushing me!)*"

I push Len down with my forepaw. Then Christina tentatively opens her mouth.

"Grrr… *(I… I…)*"

Oh, she can talk.

Len doesn't speak too highly of her, so I assumed she had low intelligence.

"Grrr…… *(I—I—I love it when Mistress steps on me…… I love being stepped on every day……)*"

So she wasn't being a footstool against her will. She was happy to serve.

"Arwf?! *(Oh no, is she a pervert?! A genuine pervert?!)*"

"Squeak. *(You're one to talk, beloved.)*"

"Bark! *(Hey! Right back atcha, perv!)*"

A dragon who loves to be stepped on by humans, a dog who loves to lick crying girls, and a thousand-year-old spinster who wants to marry a two-month-old puppy.

If we work out who the biggest pervert is, it would be…

"Arwf. *(It's clearly Len. You're the number one pervert here.)*"

Thinking about it rationally, she's definitely the most worrying out of the three of us. She's into underage beast boys who aren't even the same species as her. I have every right to kink shame.

"Squeak! *(What did you say?! How am I a pervert?! I am a pure-hearted young maiden!)*"

"Woof! Woof! *(I told you to stop poking your face out whenever you want!)*"

It looks like I'm running around chasing my tail as I argue with Len. Lady Mary probably thinks it's very strange, as she tilts her head.

"What's wrong, Routa?"

"Arwf. *(Oh, it's nothing.)*"

I somehow manage to get Len back into my mane and sit down innocently.

Lady Mary looks slightly puzzled as she pets my head.

I can see the sun through the hole in the wall that Christina made. It's about to set.

We need to get back to the inn, or Miranda and the others will worry.

"*Sniff*... Ohhh-ho-ho-ho! I have shown you something most unseemly!"

Drills wipes away her tears and stands up, laughing in that high-pitched voice with the back of her hand up to her mouth.

"And you have been here long enough! We shall call it a draw!"

Hmm, it doesn't really sound like she's learned her lesson now that she's composed herself.

"I shall see you to your inn! Be grateful of my generosity!"

With that, Drills orders the servants, who finally arrive, to clean up the room and prepare a carriage.

The servants gawk at the scene in front of them, but they quickly return to work at the sound of her high-pitched laugh.

It's not long before we're in the carriage heading back to the inn.

† † †

The magnificent horse-drawn carriage moves down the roads to the sound of hooves clopping.

Christina has to stay behind because she can't fit in the carriage.

My lady and Drills sit next to each other, buzzing with conversation once more. I'm glad they get along so well.

I-it's not like I'm feeling left out or anything like that... No, that's a lie. I really want to be involved. I want to be squished between two pretty girls. I want to be sandwiched.

How depressing. I can't even move my body in this tiny carriage.

Instead, I stick my head out of the window and enjoy the fresh air.

"Arwf. *(You really do feel the cold once it gets dark.)*"

Night completely falls outside as we're riding along in the carriage, and fragrant evening aromas fill the air.

Creamy, spicy, all sorts of smells.

I wonder what's for dinner tonight. I'm really looking forward to a high-class hotel dinner!

The carriage ride is super-smooth as we travel through the streets and eventually stop in front of an inn. Standing by the gate is a group of familiar faces waiting for us.

"We're back, Father."

My lady opens the door and leaps out of the carriage without the driver's aid.

"O-ohhh! Mary?! You're safe! You're not hurt, are you?!"

Papa spins around when she calls out to him.

"Yes! Routa and I are both fine."

"Zenobia just told us what happened. We were just about to send the guards out to find you!"

"Oh, Father, no need to make such a fuss."

Behind Papa, who now has the waterworks on full blast, are Zenobia and Miranda, who look exhausted for some reason.

The inn wasn't that far from where we left them. Why do they look so tired?

Actually, I can imagine why.

Zenobia going the wrong way; Zenobia not listening to others; Zenobia dragging Miranda around. It's all Zenobia's fault, I'm sure.

You did well to endure, Miranda.

I silently extend well-wishes to the frazzled Miranda.

"Excellent! Truly excellent! I am thankful from the bottom of my heart that your daughter is safe!"

Ever the brownnoser, the man with the curly sideburns sidles up to Papa. But he freezes the moment he sees the young lady who follows Lady Mary from the carriage.

"E-Elizabeth…?!"

"F-Father…?!"

Ah. I knew they were related. Those over-the-top curls are a dead giveaway.

"What are you doing here?!"

"Wh-what about you, Father?!"

"I was conducting important trade negotiations... How fortuitous! We might make dealings with the excellent Faulks Co.!"

"Oh, Father, all you ever talk about is work..."

Drills looks away from her excited father, saddened by more of the same.

"Wait, Faulks Co....? Huh? But that man is Mary's father, which means Mary is—"

"Is this your daughter, Mr. Morgan?"

Papa, who was practically drowning in tears a moment ago, returns to work mode and calls out to the two of them.

"It is an honor to meet you. I am Gandolf Von Faulks. You are the one who brought my daughter back to me, correct? You have my thanks."

"Wh-wh-why, yes......!"

The golden drills are spinning so much, she can't even respond with an introduction.

"Arwf. *(She finally realized.)*"

She kept calling the beloved daughter of a superrich marquis a commoner and making fun of her!

"E-Elizabeth?! Please don't tell me you were impolite to Lord Faulks's daughter......?!"

Well yeah, she called her a commoner and berated her. *Then* she took us to a room full of monsters and put her life in danger.

This must be some karmic retribution for what she's put us through! A complete role reversal!

Ha-ha-ha! Ha......ha. Hmm. Is this right...?

You'd think this would be payback to Drills since she was being such a snob, but now Lady Mary and she have become close friends, and she can't hide her pained expression.

Having the monsters she was keeping as pets break free and go on a rampage is punishment enough.

"Hmm, what's all this about, Mr. Morgan?"

"Oh, well, you see, this is, um...!"

Both father and daughter start to tremble under Papa's gaze.

My lady sees this and moves up next to Drills.

"We've become friends!"

She puts her arm around Drills's frozen shoulders, and she snaps back to reality.

"Mary…?"

"Isn't that right, Eliza? She invited me to her home, and we talked lots and lots."

Tears begin to fall from Papa's eyes again upon seeing his daughter's happy face.

"Wh-what's this? My Mary made a friend…! I see now, I see…!"

He nods, moved to tears, and grabs Morgan's shoulders.

"I cannot be more grateful to your daughter! I look forward to publicly working with you, Mr. Morgan! I accept everything discussed during our negotiations."

"R-r-really…?! You did it, Elizabeth! Well done! Now the Morgan Trading Co. is safe!"

Old man Morgan is so happy, he looks like he's about to dance, but Papa looks at him with a serious expression again.

"However. You must take care of your home from now on. It's not good to ignore your family because you are too busy. Never let yourself be caught up chasing after business."

Papa's got some sharp ears, too. He must have heard Drills's muttering before.

"Y-y-y-y-yes! Of course! I understand! I will take that to heart…!"

Looks like the negotiations went well, and their parent/child relationship will get better.

And with that, the unexpected incident in the Royal Capital comes to a close.

† † †

It's our final day in the Royal Capital.

They've come to the port to see us off.

"Maaaarrrryyyy! I shall come over to your home neeeext! I proooomiiiise!"

Drills cries out in farewell.

Things were awkward for a while once she found out that Lady Mary was of a much higher social status, but Lady Mary didn't hold it against her. After spending several days together, Drills soon opened up to her. The day before we were to leave, they hugged and cried, not wanting to leave each other.

"That's a promise! I'll send letters, too!"

Lady Mary smiles and waves. It's almost as if she's not sad at all. Because they promised to see each other again.

"Yes, indeed! I am *so* happy we became friends!"

The one who's crying the most is definitely Papa, and he nods with tears streaming down his face.

The airship creates a rush of air as it starts to float up and slowly departs from the Royal Capital.

The sight of Drills making big waves and old man Morgan panicking gets smaller and smaller.

Lady Mary waves the entire time, even when she can no longer see Drills, even when we're hidden by the clouds above the city.

"Arwf. *(Well, that really was a good trip.)*"

We made lots of great memories of our time in the Royal Capital, finishing our plans without incident.

But at that moment, there was already a new batch of trouble brewing, though I didn't know it at the time.

04 Safe Return! ...Or So I Thought, but Trouble Followed Us!

It's been three days since we got back.

My lady's excitement hasn't waned in the slightest, and she talks about Drillizabeth all the time. Even in bed! She's already started writing her letters.

As her pet, it makes me feel a little lonely, but seeing her beaming face makes it all worth it.

And it's not like Lady Mary has stopped loving me. She still pets me and spoils me every day.

"Arwf. *(And when night comes, and my lady is asleep, I can have my own fun like this.)*"

Heh-heh-heh. There's nothing better than sneaking a midnight snack.

In the dead of night when everyone in the mansion is sleeping, I tiptoe into the kitchen.

"Arwf! *(Ooh, I found you, my beautiful leg of ham. I'm sure you'll be delicious thinly sliced, but I can't wait to sink my teeth into you right this second!)*"

My razor-sharp teeth can easily slice through the evenly smoked ham. I actually love the feeling of chewing meat.

Hidden deep within the larder that chef James is in charge of, I locate my prize and secure it with my mouth.

The entire pig leg was smoked into ham, making it look like a club. It takes almost a whole year for the ham to cure, which is why this isn't a piece James made. I know this because I eat every single piece of meat that comes into the mansion.

Hee-hee-hee. The old man got furious at me once, and I went through quite the ordeal. That giant boar was terrifying.

That's why I'm pretty sure this ham is an ingredient that's brought to the mansion periodically.

The old man didn't have a hand in making it, but it's still delicious.

Of course, his selection of ingredients is top-notch, too.

"Woof, woof. *(Hee-hee-hee, the feast will be complete once* she *sneaks some booze from Papa's wine cellar.)*"

Tonight, I dine on ham and wine.

"Squeak… *(Oh, my darling, you're always doing this…)*"

The mouse sitting atop my head sighs in exasperation.

"Arwf? *(What? You got something to say?)*"

Len's always sleeping, but for once, she's awake tonight.

"Squee. *(I have much to say. I am simply too appalled for words. To think my husband would sneak around in the dead of night to steal food.)*"

Who are you calling your husband?

"Bark. *(You won't get any if you keep complaining like that.)*"

"Squeak! *(I care not for stolen goods! If you were a brave hero, you would rightfully take what is yours instead of resorting to petty thievery.)*"

Thievery seems like a harsh way to put it.

I think we're experiencing a bit of a cultural disconnect.

"Woof! Woof! *(Hey, idiot! If I did that, I'd be chased out of the mansion! And do you think I'd have a chance against old man James?! He'd fillet me like a fish in no time!)*"

I vividly remember the old man carving up the giant boar. The way he skillfully handled the knife, peeling off the armor-like fur and slicing up the meat expertly, was so…

…terrifying. I'm *way* more frightened of the old man than I am of Zenobia.

Which is why I sneak around.

"Squeak? *(How pathetic... And you call yourself a proud Fen Wolf?)*"

"Woof. *(I sure don't. I'm a dog.)*"

I am a natural-born pet, gifted with extreme laziness.

"Mrow. *(You're late, Routa. I've already completed my mission.)*"

I look in the direction of the voice and see a cat perched on the kitchen's windowsill, the moon in full view behind her.

A wine bottle and some glasses are orbiting her.

"Arwf! *(Oh! Nice one, Nahura!)*"

You're way more useful than the squeaky freeloader.

The fact that Nahura already has the booze means I was right to enlist her aid.

"Squeak! *(You're at fault, too, you bad cat! Don't you dare seduce my husband!)*"

"M-mrow! *(I-it's not what it looks like, Lady Len! Routa was the one who said we should have a party!)*"

Nahura's a cat, but she *hates* mice. Just one squeak from Len, and she jumps out of the window in fear.

"Squeak! *(Hold it! You need to be punished!)*"

"Meeeew! *(Nooo! Don't bite my eaaaars!!)*"

The two of them run around and around the tree in the middle of the garden.

"Woof, woof... *(Hey! I'm going to eat all the ham without yoooouuuu...!)*"

I watch the mouse chase the cat in the moonlit garden as I sink my teeth into the fatty ham.

Nom, nom.

Mm, it's hard and bitter.

I'm not sure if it's the curing process or what, but this ham is surprisingly tough.

Even if I bite through the skin, there's a thick layer of fat waiting for me.

"Mrow. *(Routa, biting into it like that is* so *uncivilized…meow.)*"

Why does she keep correcting herself like that? She was talking normally before.

She's meowing normally, so saying "meow" at the end of the sentence doesn't mean anything.

"Mewl. *(Ham should be eaten in thin slices that have been shaved off. If you want to eat something delicious, you need to know the best way to eat it.)*"

She kind of sounds like a gourmet.

"Mew. *(Just leave it to me.)*"

She holds up her front paw and waves it. A knife in the kitchen flies over and slices through the ham as though it's paper.

"Arwf! *(Wow! Incredible! That's amazing!)*"

"Meow. *(Hee-hee-hee. Levitating items is my specialty.)*"

She looks embarrassed as she cleans the back of her ears while the knife glides effortlessly. It slices through the skin, covered in a layer of yellow crust, proof that the ham was cured, and exposes the white layer of fat. The fat is really good, but it's finally time for the part we've been waiting for: the red meat.

Nahura painstakingly does it again, slicing the fat incredibly thinly. The red meat is slowly revealed.

"Mewl. *(The outside is smoked and cured, so it's fairly dry.)*"

"Woof, woof? *(You know your stuff. You've only just started coming to the mansion. How do you know so much?)*"

"Mrow, mew. *(I've been here plenty of times before you started living here. Mistress is Lady Mary's physician, so we've been here lots of times. I've seen Mistress and the members of this house eat this often. Hee-hee-hee. This is actually the first time I'll have this. I'm looking forward to it.)*"

As she keeps slicing through the ham, the meat slowly turns pink, revealing the moist part of the ham.

"Mewl. *(We'll eat that a little later. For now, let's enjoy the cured part of the ham.)*"

"Arwf! *(Sweet! I'm digging in!)*"

"Mew! *(No! Bad Routa!)*"

"Arww? *(Awww. I can't eat it yet?)*"

"Meow. *(Wait just a minute.)*"

I frown and try to seem dejected with my nonexistent eyebrows.

"Mewl. *(We're going to use these on the dry ham.)*"

She waves her paw again, and two bottles from the kitchen fly over. Like a couple doing the waltz, the two bottles danced around each other as their caps came off.

Clear yellow liquids dribble out.

"Arwf? *(Honey? And that's olive oil?)*"

"Mewl… *(Brilliant deduction, my dear Routa. And finally…)*"

This time, a hole opens above Nahura's head.

I recognize that ability. It's space magic.

Right as I think that, a fat jar falls out of the hole.

"Mewl. *(These are raspberries that were handpicked just this morning. They're immature, which means they'll be very sour.)*"

Sour!

She puts the bright-red raspberries on top of the ham as if she were decorating a cake.

"Mewl! *(There you go! It should be good! I think! Maybe!)*"

Oh yeah, you haven't had this before, either.

And then she casually has me taste it first to see if it's good. Very sneaky.

"Woof, woof! *(Whatever. I don't care what it'll taste like—I just want to eat it. Which I'm going to do right now!)*"

I take a number of thinly sliced pieces into my mouth and throw them in the air. Then I catch them with my mouth again and chew.

"Arwf! *(Sweet! Sour! Salty! Soooooooo goooooooood!!)*"

The dried ham has a strong saltiness, but the olive oil evens it out, giving it a very smooth taste. At the same time, the thick honey brings a very rich sweetness, but when combined with the sourness of the raspberries, the palate is blessed by a very mellow fruit flavor.

The popping sensation from the raspberries further adds to the eating experience. I'm looking forward to trying them with the drink.

The flavor is easily ten times richer and more intricate than prosciutto *e melone* from my old world.

"Arwf, arwf! *(It's insanely good! Nahura! This is seriously amazing!)*"

"Meow. *(Oh good, then I'll have some, too. Oh, drink some of this.)*"

The cork pops out of the bottle, and the wine is poured into cocktail glasses that will be easy for us to drink from.

The froth on the carbonated wine is refreshing on the tongue and exhilarating as it travels down the throat.

"Woof, woof. *(Oh, nice selection. You've got good taste. Unlike a certain freeloader.)*"

"...Squeak? *(Excuse me, did you just call me a tasteless freeloader?)*"

Len, not long for the waking world, grumbles from the top of my head.

"Woof! *(Huh? What's that? I can't hear you! It's too delicious! This ham is too good!)*"

"Meow, mrow. *(Most delicious! I can't believe Mistress would hog something so delicious. I'll never forgive her. How dare she.)*"

Nahura seethes with rage even as her mouth is full of raspberry ham.

"Woof, woof. *(Come on now, come on now. There's plenty of ham left!)*"

"Squee... *(Hmmmm...)*"

Len side-eyes the jovial Nahura and me. It doesn't look like she's going to be honest with herself, though. She's clearly interested. Okay, then. Let's nudge her a little.

"Woof, woof. *(Oh, little Len, it's such a shame you can't eat this delicious ham. Your pride won't let you forgive anyone who eats stolen food, right?)*"

"Squeak! *(E-exactly! The strong and the proud should not have to steal the things they desire! Wh-which is why...I—I don't want any! None at all!)*"

"Woof, woof! *(Oh? Really? You don't want any? Then I guess we'll just have to gobble it all up. Nahura!)*"

"Meow! *(Okaaaay!)*"

We leave Len alone and devour the raspberry ham without her.

"Arwf! *(It's so good! Delicious!)*"

"Mew! *(Mmm, truly exquisite!)*"

The cured ham disappears slice after slice.

Len simply watches us in frustration.

"S-squee... *(...Damn it. I—I don't need any of it...)*"

She begins to cry.

This thousand-year-old spinster who always acts so high-and-mighty is actually a kid deep down.

Back when I first snuck into her nest for the wyrmnil, and she tried to act so welcoming, she was probably just masking her loneliness.

Oh geez, we should probably stop bullying her.

"Woof, woof. *(Okay, I'm sorry. We'll stop teasing you. Please stop crying, Len.)*"

"Squeak! *(I-I-I'm not crying!)*"

Len snaps back even as a raspberry wrapped in a piece of ham is offered to her.

"Mew. *(Here you go, Len.)*"

This piece of meat has been cut to look like a flower.

Nahura must have used her magic to make it.

"Mrow. *(Sorry for being so mean, Lady Len. We went too far.)*"

"Squeak! *(H-hmph! It's not like I was crying or anything! I'm not even angry! Nor can it be said that I desire to have a piece, either!)*"

From the top of my head, Len makes a show of turning her head the other way, but she keeps glancing back to the ham.

She's being way too obvious.

"Mewl? *(You don't need to tell us that. But I would like you to try some. Will you humor this humble cat's request?)*"

She raises both paws in a praying motion.

Wow, she really knows how to work the cute angle.

Maybe I should start calling her Master and study under her tutelage.

"Squee? *(Hmm? R-really? I suppose I'll* have *to try some if you ask me like that. I'm willing to give it a taste, so hand it over already!)*"

"Mewl. *(Of course, here you go.)*"

The raspberry ham flower floats over to Len.

If I turn my head and snatch it right now, she'll probably never stop crying. It's pretty easy to imagine, but then I start feeling bad for her, so I drop the idea.

"Squee! *(Th-this really is delicious! No, it is beyond delicious! Your skills know no equal, Nahura!)*"

Len takes bite after bite of ham in between her blubbering.

Nahura watches her with prideful affection…

…from a good distance away.

"Woof? *(I guess you're still scared of mice, huh?)*"

Having made up, the three of us enjoy the feast together until right before dawn.

† † †

"Mew! Mew! *(Routa! Wake up! Please wake up!)*"

Someone's biting my tummy.

Mmm, too sleepy. Five more minutes.

"Squeak, squeak… *(What a disgraceful way to sleep. Showing his belly, completely defenseless, snoring loudly… I don't know if it's a show of confidence, or if I should lament that there is nary a drop of wild beast in him anywhere…)*"

"Mew! *(Routa. It's morning. The cook's going to wake up and be here any minute!)*"

"Squee. *(Just leave him be. It's his fault for not waking up sooner. I'm going back to sleep. Please roll over, beloved.)*"

Mmm, huh? I just need to roll over? Okaaaay.

I roll over in my sleep and feel something squirm into my mane.

"Squee. *(Don't say we didn't try to wake you.)*"

"Mrow! *(Well, I'm not staying around to get told off!)*"

Told off? Why?

I sense Nahura moving away, and I can feel Len's sleeping breath on my back.

It's all pretty odd, so I try to open my eyes. But it's no good. The morning light is simply too bright.

I'm pretty sure we were drinking together all night last night... but my memory's still pretty fuzzy.

Oh, right. We talked about how we needed to tidy up, or we'd get in trouble. And then...

"Arwf! *(That's right! We need to destroy the evidence!)*"

I suddenly snap awake to see—

"Hello, Routa. It sure looks like you had fun last night."

—the old man standing before me, his burly arms crossed.

"A-arwf... *(U-uh-oh...)*"

With the morning sun behind him, the old man's face is shrouded in shadow. The sight of it fills me with dread.

"You really are incorrigible. Every single day, you sneak in here to steal food, and this time wasn't like the others..."

E-eek! H-he's going to kill me.

Will this be my final day?

"I should be mad at you, but..."

He unfolds his arms and ruffles my head.

"I heard you did a great deed in the Royal Capital. You helped the young lady when she got lost, and it was thanks to you she made a friend, right?"

Huh? He's *not* mad at me?

In fact, he seems to be overjoyed.

"I was really worried about her because she didn't have any friends her age. You're a good boy, Routa. Well done."

Heh-heh-heh. It was nothing!

"I'm buying more ingredients than ever before. That means your habit of eating everything in sight shouldn't be an issue anymore. But please stop sneaking in here in the middle of the night."

"Woof! Woof! *(O-old man! How merciful you are! Truly a man among men! Pet me, pet me!)*"

I burrow my muzzle into his clothes, and he chuckles, scratching me with both hands.

"...Besides, that ham you stole was a little past its time, so I wasn't planning on serving it to the master. I think I might've found a great way to dispose of stuff like that."

Hmm? What was that?

"Come on, now. You'd best pull yourself together and go see the young lady. She'll be sad if she wakes up and you're not there."

Oh, right!

Being there when my lady wakes up is one of my small pleasures in life. I'll never let anyone take that away from me.

Today, as any other, I want to admire her adorable sleeping face.

"Woof, woof! *(I'm coming, my lady!)*"

† † †

Lady Mary's sleeping face buried in the bed is still lovely.

Her hair flows across the pillow like golden dust as she sleeps as still as a painting.

I want to crawl under the duvet and sleep with her, but it won't be long before the maid arrives with the morning tea.

"Arwf! *(My lady! It's morning!)*"

I poke her velvet skin with my nose, and she frowns before opening her eyes.

"Mmnya... Good morning, Routa..."

Now awake, Lady Mary rubs her eyes and lets out a little yawn.

"Woof! *(Good morning, my lady!)*"

"Gnh..."

I give her an energetic reply, and she hugs me tight around the neck.

"Arwf... *(Ahhh, pure bliss...)*"

Lady Mary smells amazing today, too. I want to rub my face in her hair and revel in her scent.

Actually, I'll do just that.

Sniff, sniff. Sniff, sniff.

"Hmm? Hey, Routa, you smell like alcohol..."

"Arwf?! (Haff. *Did I drink too much last night?!)*"

Lady Mary moves away.

Aw, I was sniffing that!

"Let's go to the lake this afternoon. I'm sure the smell will go away with a good swim."

"Woof, woof! *(Good idea!)*"

It's been forever since I've had the old man's sandwiches! Herb-encrusted chicken or smoked salmon between slices of colorful vegetable bread. Both options sound fantastic.

"Let's invite Dr. Hecate. Tee-hee, I'm looking forward to this afternoon now. I need to work hard and finish my studies early. Be a good boy and wait for me, okay?"

She's such a good girl.

"Arwf! *(I'll make sure I rest lots and lots to make up for how hard you're working! Just leave it to me!)*"

† † †

A carriage drawn by two horses nimbly makes its way down the forest road.

It should be hotter now that it's midday, but the carriage's interior is surprisingly pleasant and cool. The strong summer sun is blocked by the tops of the trees covering the road. The air, thick with oxygen, carries the strong smell of the foliage.

"Excuse me, my lady. But don't you think Routa has gotten larger?"

Miranda, sitting opposite Lady Mary, voices her suspicion while looking right at me.

"Arwf! *(H-ha-ha-ha! Oh, you! It's just your imagination.)*"

I look off in a random direction and try to make myself small.

Crap, even Miranda's catching on.

"Really? Well, he is a growing boy!"

Lady Mary hugs me tight.

Oh, my lady. Her pure heart allows her to see the best in anyone.

I hope she always stays this way.

She squeezes herself next to me, completely infatuated with my fluffy fur.

This carriage is huge, but it's quite cramped for me. Even now, my lady doesn't seem to mind the tight squeeze and would rather stay close to me.

"You really love Routa, don't you, Mary? I'm so jealous."

Hecate, sitting opposite me, tickles my nose with her fingers.

Stop. I'm going to sneeze.

Uh-oh, here it comes.

"GAFUU!!"

I shove my head out of the window and sneeze loudly.

Ew, snot.

"Honestly, what *are* you doing?"

I look over in the direction of the voice to see Zenobia driving the carriage.

She's leaning forward with a fed-up expression, holding out a handkerchief to me.

"Here, don't move. I'll wipe it off."

Having the snot wiped away makes me feel much better.

"Woof. *(Thanks, Zenobia.)*"

"D-don't get the wrong idea. I can't have you besmirching the Faulks family name with such a crude display."

Zenobia looks away and goes back to driving the carriage.

Ah, what a perfect *tsundere.*

Don't worry—I know how you really feel. I see you getting jealous whenever my lady pets me.

Come on, Zenobia. Ditch the sword and come get some cuddles.

"Arwf. *(Mmm, the air feels so good. Looks like we're going to have good weather today.)*"

I can't smell any monsters in the forest, either.

Looks like the monsters Nahura teleported here are keeping their promise. And Garo and the other wolves are doing their jobs, too.

I wonder if they're off hunting bad monsters again today.

I haven't seen them in a while. Maybe I'll bring them a gift tonight.

† † †

The carriage stops under a large tree, and I sit and wait like a good boy.

"A swimsuit?"

I can hear Miranda on the other side of the carriage.

Hecate had summoned all the ladies as soon as we arrived at the lake.

"That's right. It's something you wear when you go swimming. I just happened to find these in the Royal Capital and ended up buying them."

"E-even so, isn't this practically underwear...?!"

I can tell Zenobia's lost for words.

What kind of swimsuits did she give them? My imagination is going crazy.

"But you're naked in the bath."

"Yes, but this is outdoors..."

"We're the only ones here. There's nothing to worry about."

She's really pushing this.

"Mrow. *(Mistress is lying about accidentally finding them. She went out with the express purpose of purchasing swimsuits for today. She even went to a designer store and picked those out at a crazy-ridiculous price.)*"

I look up to see a crimson cat lying on a branch above me.

"Arwf. *(Oh, hey, Nahura.)*"

I didn't think she was in the carriage. When did she get here?

"Mew. *(I can appear anywhere you are, Routa.)*"

Levitation and teleportation. Man, Nahura's magic really is useful.

"Mew, mrow. *(I wouldn't say Mistress is vain, just that she isn't honest with herself. She's lived so long, I don't think she really knows how to connect with people anymore. Like when a grandma wants to play with her grandchildren, but she can't seem to make it work. She doesn't have anything to talk to them about, so she bribes them instead.)*"

"Woof... *(You know, if you say stuff like that...)*"

"Urk! *(...Arwl?! N-no, Mistress! It just slipped out...! Oh no! Please no! Don't put tentacles in my tummy...!)*"

I'm assuming Hecate's talking to her telepathically just as Nahura faints in the tree above.

Wait, did she say "tentacles"? Nahura's body sure is terrifying. She looks like a cat, but she's actually a homunculus. I wonder what kind of magic was used to make her.

Would something jump out if someone cut her belly open? I can't imagine anything but horrors.

"*I'm ready!*"

I hear my lady's musical voice in the middle of Hecate and Zenobia's discussion.

She leaps out from the shadow of the carriage.

"What do you think, Routa? Does it suit me?"

She spins around, showing off her aqua bikini, then leans over. She tucks her long, flowing blond hair behind her ears and smiles a little in embarrassment—it's wonderful.

"Woof! Woof! *(It really, really suits you! You're* so *cute!)*"

If I wasn't a dog, I'd get down on one knee and propose to her here and now.

My lady is so cute. She's the cutest in the whole wide world.

"Squeak?! *(D-does my darling...?! No, they're different species. He would never...)*"

I'm guessing Len's finally woken up, since I can hear her complaining on my back.

I'll just ignore her. I want to savor this sight even for just a moment longer.

"There's no way to fasten it, Ms. Miranda. I can't believe we let the young lady wear something like this..."

"Y-you're right. We must steel ourselves."

I hear the rustling of fabric for a few minutes before the other two ladies step out from behind the carriage.

Miranda looks embarrassed as she holds her arms beneath her chest, and Zenobia stands menacingly.

They're both wearing bikinis as revealing as Lady Mary's.

Miranda's white swimsuit is a band around the chest, almost resembling a pareo's fabric. The bottom part is a sarong with large colorful flowers painted across it. It really serves to show off the beauty of the flower normally hidden away by propriety.

Zenobia's swimsuit is an even brighter red than her golden-copper hair. There's a frilly decoration on the chest that seems to have offset her aggressive personality, causing her to show a more girlie side than usual.

What a sight for sore eyes. They're both so gorgeous. What is this, paradise?

Hecate, how could you let me see such beauties?

"O-oh my. What's wrong, Routa? You're staring."

"D-don't stare... Dummy."

Their embarrassed faces are to die for.

Even if my tongue lolls out, I'm just a dog! There's nothing suspicious about that!

"It takes a surprisingly long time to put these on, doesn't it?"

Hecate, the star of the show, appears at last.

Her long silver hair flows behind her as she struts over. It isn't long before I become fixated on one generous detail.

Her cups runneth over.

One more time for emphasis.

Her cups runneth *over*!

I thought about this when we were in the bath, but Hecate has a really impressive body. Her small frame and pale skin look incredibly

soft. Her black string bikini presses into her supple flesh in all sorts of wonderful ways, creating a sensational atmosphere.

It's incredibly sexy.

That swimsuit is bound to come off if she actually tries swimming in it. I have a feeling it's meant to be used for something else.

"Meow... *(That outfit looks absolutely lecherous...)*"

Nahura, who's barely hanging on to life at this point, says something unnecessary again.

Hecate flashes her a look, and Nahura stiffens as if she were struck by electricity before falling off the branch.

"I'll punish you later, Nahura. What about you, Routa? Do *you* have something to say?"

Why don't you act your age?

Yeah right, if I said that, I'd be pulverized.

Not that I'd ever think that in the first place.

"A-arwf. *(You truly are a feast for the eyes. My sincerest thanks.)*"

I'm so glad I'm a dog.

Really glad.

I'll never forget this view for the rest of my life.

It will be a treasured memory locked away in my brain for all eternity.

"Squea...! *(B-beloved, you really are...!)*"

Len's voice trembles in shock.

"Squeak! *(I was thinking* No, it cannot be...! *But are you attracted to these...these* humans*...?!)*"

Yeah, I am—what about it?

"Squeak?! Squeak?! *(Why?! You don't react to my glorious blue scales but find these scaleless females* attractive*?!)*"

"Arwf. *(I don't think scales are sexy. I have high standards. Come back when you've grown some boobs.)*"

Besides, you're a mouse right now.

Either way, I'm not interested.

"Squeak! *(Uuuuugh!! You are unbelievable! So incredibly frustrating!)*"

"Arwf?! *(Ow! Hey! Don't bite me! That hurts! That really hurts!)*"

"Squee! Squee! *(I won't forgive you! I won't allow this! Not while you have meeeeeeeeeeeeee!!)*"

"Arwwww! *(Owwwwwwwwwwwwwwww!)*"

Len bites me so hard, I start to bleed, while Nahura remains knocked out under the tree.

† † †

The sunlight reflecting off the lake is blinding, but the shallow water is still cold.

"Woof? *(Hey, Len. How long are you gonna sulk for?)*"

"Squee. *(…I'm not sulking.)*"

Len the blue mouse puffs out her cheeks as she nibbles on a sandwich crumb.

She's *really* in a mood.

"Arwf… *(Don't be like that; let's make up…)*"

I leave her on top of my head as I dog-paddle in the lake.

She bit me a lot, but I try to cheer her up like she's a trained horse.

"Squeak, squeak. *(You shouldn't look at other women. I can understand other Fen Wolves, but human females…? You're perverted even for perverts. I can't help but think you're seriously ill.)*"

Yeah, well, I'm not a furry.

Just because I'm a dog now doesn't mean you can rope me into that lifestyle.

If anything, *you're* a dragon, but you've fallen for a Fen Wolf. I want an hour-long cross-examination to see if you're the bigger pervert.

"Squeak. *(Well anyway, I have come up with a secret plan to fix this. Look forward to that, my darling.)*"

Len snorts as she laughs, her confidence renewed.

"Bark? *(Hmm? What's that?)*"

"Squeak! *(You'll know when it happens!)*"

"Arwf! *(Whatever. I'm just happy you're feeling better. Let's head back to shore!)*"

"Squeak. *(Oh no! Oh no! I'm rather enjoying our boat ride.)*"

"Bark. *(Boat ride? I* am *the boat.)*"

I'm getting a little tired from swimming around. I think I ate too many sandwiches, and I'm starting to cramp up.

I look over to the shore to see my lady and the others taking a post-lunch break.

Everyone is napping on the reclining chairs Hecate brought.

A large parasol is open above them, making it look like they're at a resort.

My lady has Nahura on her tummy, gently running her fingers through her fur. She tickles her under the chin and strokes her tail from base to tip. Nahura is putty in her hands, likely because she doesn't usually get this kind of treatment from Hecate.

Just look at that face. She's practically melting.

Damn, I'm jealous. I want Lady Mary to pet me, too!

Damn that Nahura. She just looked over at me with her "I win" face.

"Woof! *(Grrr, I should be the one getting petted! Damn you, Nahura! Teach me your ways!)*"

A cute pose! I need to come up with a pose so cute it'll fry my lady's brain!

"Squee… *(You're staring at that female again… Don't tell me you're into children, too… If you have interest even in the children of other species, you truly are the pervert of perverts.)*"

Speak for yourself. You've been going after a child of another species this whole time.

"Woof. *(You don't get it. I don't think of my lady that way.)*"

I am not sexually attracted to Lady Mary at all. What I feel for her is pure.

If I have to put it in words, I guess she's more like a guardian?

She gives me a life free of hardship, and she pampers me as much as I want.

She's like a mother to me!

"Squeak… *(…You really are creepy…)*"

Len is really good at bringing out unpleasant feelings.

Hey, Len. Aren't you being a little harsh for someone who's supposed to be in love with me?

Calling someone creepy would normally hurt their feelings.

† † †

Our break time at the lake comes to an end, and we get back in the carriage and return to the mansion.

"Hmm? Who are those people?"

I hear Zenobia murmur from the driver's seat.

I stick my head out of the window and look in the direction we're heading.

I can see the mansion gate ahead of us. It looks like a heated conversation is unfolding between a group of men in travelers' clothes and one of the mansion's servants.

"That's what I'm saying! This forest is Faulks property! You cannot enter without the master's permission!"

The only one standing up against these men is one of the maids.

She's short, but she doesn't seem intimidated, even though she's outnumbered. She's small, but she's standing tall, her hands on her hips and her chest puffed out, though something about her appearance still lacks impact.

Perhaps it's because of her black pigtails, but she looks incredibly young.

"Arwf! *(Wait, that's Toa!)*

The one who falls down when she sees me? The two-time champion of making me want to lick her crying face? *That* Toa?

"And we're saying we're here to get that permission!"

"But the master is in the middle of work! You need to make an appointment and come back another day!"

The little maid firmly replies to the angry men.

"It's a half-day trip to the nearest village! You want us to go back there?! Look! This is permission from the guild! This is an official investigation!"

"Even if you have permission from the guild, they have no jurisdiction over this household! If you mean to follow proper procedures, you must turn back, now!"

Wow—go, Toa. She doesn't seem the least bit threatened.

But those men have swords on their hips, and the redness of their red faces suggests they're down to their last straw. It would be best to not aggravate them.

"Look, borders are pointless! Let us through! He'll understand once he hears us out!"

"W-wait—!"

They knock the little maid down as they shove their way past.

"Arwf! *(Uh-oh, that's not good!)*"

I quickly open the door, leap out of the carriage, and am near the adventurers in an instant, catching Toa just before she hits the ground.

"Arwf? *(Heh-heh-heh, my fluffy body sure is useful, huh?)*"

Even Drills can confirm my cushy body's usefulness for catching people.

"Woof, woof! *(Hey, now! What are you doing to our maid?! The only one who's allowed to scare her is me!)*"

The adventurers jump back in surprise when I bark.

"Wha—?! What is that thing?!"

"A monster?! Where did it come from?!"

"Did you see that speed?! It was a total blur!"

Oh, crap! I dashed over, but that made me stand out way too much.

They're convinced I'm a monster… Wh-wh-wh-what do I do?!

"You guys! What's going on over there…?"

A less-than-impressive woman's voice causes the men to spin around.

Standing there is fiery-haired Zenobia.

"What gives you the right to raise your hand to one of the Faulks family maids…?!"

Whoa, Zenobia's furious.

Her golden-copper hair is standing on end like a lion's mane.

She's scary when she's serious.

"Wh-what?! We were sent by the guild to investigate the forest! We have official permission!"

"The guild…?"

Her eyes narrow, causing the strong men to take a step back.

The men, once awash with murderous intent, are now speechless, a cold sweat dripping from each of their brows.

"C-Captain, who is this woman…?!"

"I—I think she's… No, it can't be…!"

"Zenobia! There's no mistaking it… This is Zenobia Lionheart!"

"Zenobia? You mean *that* Zenobia…?!"

Former SS Rank. Slayer of One Thousand Men. Fortress Destroyer. Labyrinth Annihilator. The Blood-Soaked Knight with the Heart of a Lion.

Those are some ostentatious names, but they dribble out of the men's mouths in quick succession.

Wait, is Zenobia really that well-known as an adventurer? What happened to the useless knight who's so quick to cry…?

"I don't remember such paltry titles, but if you mean to bring harm to any member of this household, then you can become rust on my blade…!"

"Come on now, that's enough."

Just as Zenobia is about to unsheathe her sword, a voice stops her.

Everyone turns to the tranquil masculine voice.

"M-Master!"

The master of the house, Lord Gandolf Von Faulks, or as I like to call him, Papa, appears with servants in tow.

"I'll listen to what you have to say. Zenobia, Toa, I'm sorry you were troubled by this incident."

"O-oh, not at all!"

"Master, please excuse my behavior!"

He smiles at the two of them. He's so dignified. This is completely different from the times he's broken down crying when Hecate stole wine from his wine cellar.

"Oh my, they arrived a lot sooner than Emerada said they would… Still, this is perfect timing."

Hecate murmurs to herself, a finger pressed to her lips.

"Woof? *(What do you mean, 'perfect timing'?)*"

"Oh, the perfect time for a drink, of course!"

For you, that's all the time.

Papa, looks like the greedy witch is after your wine cellar again.

My wordless warning fails to reach Papa as he leads the four adventurers into the mansion.

Since the adventurers' business has nothing to do with us, we return to our afternoon plans.

Little did I know that the adventurers' business had *everything* to do with me.

"Arwf, arwf! *(Yum! So tasty!)*"

Today's snack is marinated beef shank broiled in wine. The beef was stir-fried with olive oil and onions, then cooked in a pan with the wine just barely covering it. The juices from the marinating period were added back in as it cooked for another two hours.

This is one of the great things about the old man's cooking. He was able to make the tough shank soft and incredibly flavorful.

He added thick-cut boiled vegetables to a pan and left them in the cooler overnight. This made the meat even softer with the umami from the broth permeating right through to the core.

The next day, it was reheated and served.

Despite the number of steps that went into crafting this masterpiece, it's given to the dog as a snack. This is why I'll never give up the pampered pooch life.

"Omff, gromff. *(The tender meat and succulent vegetables are* so *good!)*"

I'm by the back door of the kitchen like always, enjoying the meal piled high on my plate.

"Squeak… *(My darling, you* just *had a sandwich for lunch, and now you're eating again? And a huge amount, at that…)*"

"Woof! *(I'm a growing boy! It's fine! Besides, you're eating it, too!)*"

"Squeak. *('Tis but a taste. Just a taste. You need not be so stingy, beloved.)*"

"Mrow! *(Wow! You're right! You don't even have to chew! It just melts in your mouth! Delicious!)*"

"Woof, woof! *(Hey, I told you to stop swiping my meals!)*"

Hey, owner! Feed your cat properly! She only ever appears when I'm eating!

My portions keep getting smaller and smaller!

"Mrow. *(Oh, don't worry about me. I always eat properly before I come here.)*"

"Woof! *(Then stop eating my food!)*"

The three of us argue as we scramble for the meal prepared by the old man.

""""""…………………""""""

Four people are looking at us.

It's the adventurers, who have finished their meeting with Papa.

They're sitting frozen on the edge of the back garden, staring at us and trying not to drool.

"C-Captain… He's eating better food than we are…"

"It smells so good… I would even be willing to eat these claylike provisions if they smelled half as good…!"

"Maybe they'll give us some; I'd even be happy with scraps… By the way, what in the world is that? They said it was a dog, but there's no way that's true, right?"

"Just shut up and finish your food. You can eat once this investigation is over. Let's get the tent set up and go to sleep. We leave before dawn."

The men sigh deeply as they chew on what looks like dry bread.

"Captain, shouldn't we have accepted the marquis's kind offer? He said he would have dinner and rooms prepared for us..."

"Don't be ridiculous. We're here for an emergency investigation for the guild, and he gave us permission even though we forced our way in. We shouldn't abuse his generosity any more than we already have. Borrowing his garden to camp in is more than enough."

The one they call Captain chokes down some water from a flask.

"Besides, I hadn't planned to get on *Zenobia's* bad side. We'll need to report that to the guild leader when we get back."

"That's the first time I've seen that. Who would have thought we'd run into Zenobia Lionheart all the way out here?"

"They say it's a pastime for the upper class to feed and lodge artisans and adventurers, but I never expected the storied hero to force herself on some nobles."

"Well, even if she is the first adventurer to climb to the SS Rank based on *fighting ability alone*, that doesn't make her any less strange. Come to think of it, pretty much every adventurer S Rank and above is a weirdo. No one can comprehend what goes on in their heads."

"So the rumors are true? Is it true that she can't do anything but fight, has a profoundly terrible sense of direction, and always manages to cause great misfortune for nonparty members even if they've only popped into the woods for a piss?"

"Those are just exaggerations. Nothing more than outlandish rumors spread by those who are jealous of her success. If any of that were actually true, she wouldn't even be able to function in her day-to-day life."

Ha-ha-ha! The adventurers chortle.

I'm so sorry, fellas... All of that is 100 percent true.

Zenobia's sense of direction is horrible. And she's so sure of herself that she'll continue in the wrong direction forever if no one intervenes. She probably never even realizes she's lost.

"Arwf. *(I'm stuffed.)*"

"Mew. *(Me too. Ahhh, that was so good.)*"

"Squee. *(Honestly, you eat much too much, belov—* Urp.*)*"

Once we've finished our meal, Nahura, Len, and I collapse into a pile of laziness.

It doesn't matter if we look like lazy good-for-nothings. No one's going to tell us off. Just another perk of being a pet.

Until someone's shadow falls on me.

It's Toa, black pigtails in tow.

She has a large wash basket in her arms and looks down at me with a serious expression.

Did she come out here to get the laundry?

"…………"

She remains quiet, pursing her lips as she peers at me.

"Arwf? (*What's wrong?*)"

She doesn't seem angry. She seems like she wants something.

Lying on my side, I'm gazing up at her when suddenly, it hits me.

Oh, I got it. You're scared of those adventurers.

She probably wasn't scared of the adventurers at the gate because she was more concerned about appearing professional.

She looks like a child, so she's probably often treated like one.

Of course she'd be scared after being surrounded and then getting pushed over by those burly men.

She's worried they'll get in her way when she's all alone out here with the laundry.

"Arwf. *(Okay, Toa. I get what you're trying to say. Just leave it to me.)*"

I get up and conceal Toa from the adventurers. This way, she won't be able to see the adventurers, and all they'll be able to see are her feet.

I feel like this is the first time my body's size is actually useful for something.

"Th-thanks…"

She practically whispers it.

"Arwf. *(No problem.)*"

But I'm going to run for it if they do decide to mess with us. You better not expect me to fight or anything. I'm scared of them, too. They're all muscly.

"I'll be quick."

"Arwf. *(Don't worry about it. Take your time. This lazy hound has nothing better to do.)*"

I walk with her, acting as a shield, over to the washing line near the adventurers.

"H-hey, you!"

Wait. They're suddenly picking a fight?!

"Get away from her!"

"Arwf?! *(Who? Me?!)*"

I thought Papa told them about me!

"Don't pretend you didn't see us, you monster! Get away from the girl!"

"Wh-what do you want this time?! Do you have a problem with our dog?!"

Hiding behind me, Toa raises her voice.

I'm sure she's terrified, but she moves to my side to protect me and puffs out her chest.

I can see her legs shaking, but she carries herself with authority.

"Don't say something so foolish. How is this giant beast a dog…?"

"I've never seen such a huge, terrifying dog before!"

"Miss, please step away from it and come here. He's clearly a monster…!"

The adventurers are wary of me and aren't stepping any closer.

Toa, struck by their words, glares back at them with tears in her eyes.

"Routa… Routa isn't a monster!"

Toa protests, clinging on to my fur with a trembling hand so she doesn't fall over.

It's okay, Toa. You're not alone.

Their weapons are aimed at me, so even *my* legs are trembling like a baby deer's.

"Routa is the young lady's, this household's, precious dog!"

T-Toa…! You're such a good girl…! Such a good, good girl…!

You're terrified, but you still spoke on my behalf!

"Woof! Woof! *(Yeah! I'm their pet! Which means I'm Faulks property, got it?! It'll be bad if you lay a hand on me, got it?! You'll pay, got it?! Your monthly income doesn't even come close to how much you'll pay, right?!)*"

I bark with all my might, even as I lie belly-up in total submission.

"Squee……? *(Should you really be issuing such a threat, beloved…?)*"

It's fine.

Besides, they don't understand what I'm saying.

I'm just channeling my doggy appeal by looking submissive and barking.

"C-Captain. If it really is this mansion's dog, then we can't touch it…"

"Tch. Fine, then. Put your weapons away. This monster… This dog isn't threatening anyone."

The adventurers put their weapons away as their captain commands.

"I just don't understand nobles… That dog must be pretty strong."

"I guess there's no problem if it's tame."

"I've never heard of a monster being tamed by humans, though."

Uwah, they still suspect me.

I hope they don't report me along with Zenobia…

In the end, there is one hiccup, but I complete my role as Toa's shield, and she finishes collecting the laundry.

"Oh, Routa. You don't need to wait for me. This is my job, after all."

"Arwf. *(It's fine; don't worry about it.)*"

I take the surprisingly heavy basket in my mouth and head for the back door.

"Wait a minute, miss."

A voice calls out from behind, causing Toa to jump and hide behind me.

"Wh-what is it?"

"Well. We're sorry for what happened at the gate. We'll be out of your hair by tomorrow. I know we scared you, but please don't be afraid of us."

The captain bows his head in apology.

Hmm. He doesn't seem like a bad guy.

I guess it's not impossible for a large man to lower his head to a servant in this world. And I suppose he did make an honest attempt to save her before.

He might look scary, but he's a good guy.

"Arwf. *(Maybe the two of us aren't so different.)*"

"Squee… *(I'm not even going to comment…)*"

Maybe I should go to the forest tonight and talk to Garo and the others before tomorrow.

Which reminds me… The whole reason the adventurers are here in the first place is to investigate something in the forest.

05 Conducting a Peaceful Investigation! ...Or So I Thought, but I Was Wrong!

We leave the mansion in the dead of night and head deep into the forest.

"Squeak. *(What are they after? They probably wish to investigate the remains of our battle.)*"

The blue mouse Len rides atop my head, casually answering my question.

"Woof? *(The remains of our fight? You mean your nest behind that huge waterfall?)*"

"Squea. *(That's right. It's because of the high level of magic used when you and I clashed. It's caused the magic concentration in the area to rise.)*"

Hmm? Hecate and Chief Emerada mentioned something like that in the Royal Capital. I don't really remember it, though.

"Bark? *(What happens when the concentration of magic increases?)*"

"Squea. *(Nothing good if you leave it alone. The surrounding ecosystem goes crazy, and labyrinths may appear. If the magic doesn't disperse, then it could coalesce and create a powerful monster.)*"

"Bark. *(What? That sounds like a problem.)*"

"Squee. *(That's probably what those humans are here to investigate. We did emit a lot of magic. As long as they travel with a mage, they'll be able to observe from a distance.)*"

Oh, I see—they talked about that, too.

So those adventurers they mentioned being on a special investigation…would be these guys.

It's been less than two weeks since my fight with Len in the cave.

From the time they first detected the phenomenon to identifying the point of origin, getting the best adventurers for the job, and dispatching them all the way out here. All of that must have taken about ten days.

That's a speedy reaction. This world's reaction time is impressive.

"Squeak? *(Hmm, but our magic combining and creating a monster… Would it be going too far to think of it as our child?)*"

Yes.

That would be going much too far.

Wouldn't that be on the same level as immaculate conception? Just ignore it, Routa.

"Arwf? *(Could any of those terrible things have happened already?)*"

"Squea. *(No, not yet. Just because the magic concentration is high doesn't mean anything would have happened this soon. If the magic disperses, then it would take even longer for a monster to appear.)*"

"Woof. *(All right, then we'll go disperse it. ASAP.)*"

"Squeak! *(What?! You want to murder our child before it's even born?! No! I want to keep it!)*"

"Woof! *(Whoa! This conversation just went from zero to one hundred in no time at all! All I'm saying is that we need to take care of the potential threat before it becomes a problem!)*"

And please don't call it "our child"!

I haven't even done anything yet, but I'm already feeling really conflicted!

"Awoooooo! *(Come on out, you guys!)*"

I summon the Fen Wolves from my usual cliff. As usual, they show up immediately.

I look at the pack orderly lined up under the giant crescent moon.

It's a spectacular sight.

It doesn't look like everyone is here, but seeing a few hundred Fen Wolves lined up like trained soldiers makes me think they'll be a force to be reckoned with.

"Grwl! *(Attention! The king is to appoint us with a mission! Be grateful for the opportunity to serve!)*"

The wolves all stand at attention at Garo's order, and their eyes focus on me.

"Squeak. *(Mwa-ha-ha, this is more like it. It feels pretty good to stand next to my darling, who has so many retainers serving him.)*"

"Next to"? You're sitting on my head.

"Bark. *(Hey, thanks for coming, everyone. I have some introductions to make before we get started.)*"

The Fen Wolves hang on my every word.

"Squeak. *(Hmph, an introduction? Then it is important that they see me as I truly am. Very well. I grant them the privilege of laying eyes upon my resplendent visage.)*"

Len leaps high off the top of my head and transforms.

The tiny mouse spins around a few times midair and, a moment later, has turned into a giant blue dragon. Her massive wings flap once, and she lands behind me.

The Fen Wolves stir at the sight of the giant that suddenly appears before them.

"Grwl…?! *(A d-dragon…?! The king has subdued a dragon and made it serve him…?!)*"

Garo's astonishment is matched by a number of the wolves crying "Long live the king!" but I'll ignore it for now.

"Woof. *(Nahura, are you there? You should come out, too.)*"

"Mrow! *(Okaaaay, here I come!)*"

When I call her, a hole appears in the air, and out pops a crimson cat.

She gently lands on the ground next to me as if she weighs nothing at all.

"Grwl. *(Tch, it's you, Nahura.)*"

"Mew! *(Oh, Garo. Long time no see!)*"

Seems like Garo and Nahura know each other. Maybe it's from their mutual interactions with Hecate?

"Woof. *(Looks like you already know at least one of them, but let me introduce them to you anyway. The big one behind me is Lenowyrm. The cat next to me is Nahura.)*"

Len poses arrogantly, and Nahura snuggles up to me.

"GROOAR. *(I'm his wife.)*"

"Meow. *(And I'm his lover. ♪)*"

A stir runs through the crowd of Fen Wolves at this misunderstanding.

"G-grwl?! *(You have a queen and a mistress of different speciiiiieeeees?!)*"

A brown-furred wolf leaps forward.

It's Garo's aide, Bal.

We met during the incident with the boar.

"Grwl! Grwl! *(Your Majesty! What is the meaning of this?! Your betrothed should clearly be Lady Garo! How can you be dissatisfied with the strong and beautiful princess?!)*"

That's because I'm *really* not a furry.

Not that they'll understand what I'm talking about, so I don't say anything.

Garo's spirit has already left her body from shock. I'd feel bad if I did any more damage.

"Woof, woof. *(Wait, Bal. These two are just joking. Don't take them seriously.)*"

"GROOAR. *(It is no jest. I am truly serious.)*"

"Mew. *(I can tell it's what Routa truly wants.)*"

It's really not what I want; *please* shut up.

Please don't make them regret following me.

"Woof. *(That is absolutely not it. These two are my* friends. *I don't want any fighting. Any talks of wives or anything is ridiculous. Ignore them.)*"

"......Grwl. *(...Understood. I believe you, Your Highness...)*"

Bal doesn't seem convinced, but he accepts my explanation anyway and returns to the line.

"Woof. *(Well, now that that's settled, Garo, let's have a chat.)*"

Garo returns to her senses when I call out to her.

"Grwl! *(Huh?! Attention! The king is to appoint us with a mission! Be grateful for the opportunity to serve!)*"

She barks the exact same command as before.

Apparently, Garo intentionally forgot everything that just happened. I think she wiped the last few minutes from her memory.

"Woof. *(The truth is, humans will soon enter the forest. Four of them.)*"

"Grwl! *(And you want us to kill them all! Of course, my king! Leave it to us! We Fen Wolves pride ourselves on devouring our prey until not even the bones remain!)*"

"Woof! Woof! *(No! No! No! No! I'm telling you* not *to lay a paw on them!)*"

Seriously, their extreme bloodlust is going to cause problems one day.

Their "Kill all humans!" mentality is terrifying.

I'm going to have to feed them the old man's food again and remind them of how wonderful humans are.

Old man James's cooking is the foundation for peace.

"Woof, woof. *(They just need to make sure there's nothing weird going on in the forest, and then they'll leave.)*"

If they do identify an issue within the forest, then I'm sure more adventurers will come. And that'll be the end of my peaceful pet life.

I'll be stripped of my pet status and downgraded to monster. I can't let that happen, no matter what.

"Woof, woof! *(Your mission is to escort them. Give them full protection without them noticing.)*"

"Grwl... *(Yes, if my king commands...)*"

The general mood seems to be "It's unpleasant to have humans doing as they please in our territory," but they'll simply have to put up with it.

It's all for the greater good of the forest.

Everyone has to pool their strengths and work together!

"GRAR... *(This is clearly for your own selfish reasons.)*"

"Mrow. *(You really are a simple creature, Routa.)*"

Shut up.

I'll just ignore those two smart-asses.

Woof. *(All right then, now for the plan name.)*"

I pause for effect and raise my commanding voice.

"Woof! *(Commence Operation "They Thought It Was Going to Be a Lengthy Investigation, but It Turned Out to Be a Super-Easy Bath Trip. Drip, Drop"!!)*"

† † †

Dawn hasn't even broken yet when the party of A-Rank adventurers packs away their camp and sets off on their forest investigation.

In the early summer, the trees are thick with leaves, so the moonlight doesn't reach the forest floor.

Their way is lit only by the lanterns on their hips.

"Captain, we seem to be on the right path. The large amount of magical damage that the Institute of Magical Research detected is still strong. The Magic Dowsing Stone is pointing straight north."

The way is led by a man holding the small device that points them in the right direction. He has both a short and long dagger on the back of his waist and a soft leather hood over his head. The entire party is equipped with mostly lightweight armor for long-distance travel, but his clothes are especially light.

He has likely reduced his weight as much as possible so he can do his job as a ranger.

"This forest has been unexplored for a thousand years. I've heard that no monsters appear because of the sacred lake, but be on your guard anyway. There must be a powerful monster residing here for that much magical damage to occur."

The captain with a claymore on his back follows shortly behind.

He's a beefy guy standing at an impressive height. He's probably a swordsman.

The man behind the captain nods in response to his warning.

"Good point. We're a well-balanced party for clearing labyrinths and exploring new regions, but we're all A-Rank adventurers. I think they expected us to have a few encounters when they sent us here."

This man, wearing a priestlike robe and cape, checks the spiked club he's holding. His skinny frame makes him look more like a librarian than an adventurer.

"Well, a monster that spawns from a labyrinth's magic is one thing, but one that appears aboveground shouldn't be difficult."

The man with a short pike pipes up from the back of the group.

"You should stay on guard anyway. You can't rely on talent alone."

The deep-voiced lancer suddenly scrunches up his face.

"Captain, we've got company. Five hundred paces that way, but it's heading this way."

"You've got good ears, but we're not changing course. The objective point is our priority. We'll head in a straight line and eliminate anything we come across."

"Yes, sir."

"Understood."

"Got it."

They ready their weapons, and the captain nods at his stalwart companions.

The adventurers continue cautiously but without letting their speed waver.

Only a few dozen steps from the enemy.

Now that they're closer, they can sense it's a vicious creature.

"We might have some trouble with this one..."

Just as the ranger leading the way groans—the forest trembles.

In the blink of an eye, they sense a strong murderous intent, and then their adversary's aura vanishes.

"Wha—?!"

What just happened?

Right as they were about to come into contact with the source, it simply vanished.

Maybe it cloaked its presence?

No, were that the case, it would have done so earlier. It's impossible for a creature to hide its aura this close up unless it's a creature of incredible power.

And what was that aura of murderous intent that seemed to make the entire forest tremble…?

"What just happened?!"

"I don't know. Let's press on!"

The adventurers pick up the pace and head to the location where the enemy should be.

They flatten grass, squeeze past trees, and trample roots, but when they finally arrive, there's nothing there. Not even a trace of the enemy that should have been there. An ominous breeze blows through the forest.

"C-Captain…"

"Don't panic. There really is something in this forest… Stay on your guard, everyone."

The adventurers all gulp as they start to have second thoughts about this investigation.

† † †

"Arwf. *(Good, good. Everything is proceeding according to plan. Excellent, excellent.)*"

I nod at how well things are going as I watch the adventurers advancing with their weapons drawn.

The Fen Wolves have currently surrounded the adventurers, acting as their secret bodyguards. The rigorous guard of a few hundred wolves is so great that not a single monster can get in.

Even the monster that appeared before was swiftly taken care of by Garo's unit.

It was devoured in seconds.

Not a single cry was heard, nor was there any leftover gore to examine.

Impressive as always. The adventurers should be able to continue their investigation in total safety.

I also asked Garo about the monsters we released from Drills's place, and if she accidentally hunted them, but it seems they successfully relayed my message to her and are now living peacefully elsewhere in the forest.

It appears they've taken a liking to a forest rich with magic and lacking in enemies, and they won't be coming this way at all.

"Squeak. *(I see. I understand your plan now, my darling. You want a land where these humans do not come in contact with even a single monster.)*"

"Woof. *(Exactly. If we can keep them from running into any monsters, then those guys should go home quickly, right?)*"

"Mrow. *(And while that happens, our secret plan is to go on ahead to the waterfall and disperse the magic.)*"

Exactly. For once, we're all on the same page.

Now the adventurers can enjoy a safe journey.

I'll need to prepare a wonderful surprise along the way.

At their current pace, we're sure to arrive at the waterfall way before them, but I might have to set some extra time aside just in case.

"Woof! *(All right then, we're going on ahead. I'm leaving the adventurers' well-being in your paws, everyone!)*"

""""Grwl! *(Just leave it to us, O king!)*""""

I call to the Fen Wolves behind me and then head off to execute the next phase of the plan.

Shadows. All they see are shadows.

The moment they get close to sensing a monster, merciless shadows fly by.

When they finally get to the spot where the monster is supposed to be, they find nothing.

An ominous feeling washes over them, and they're stricken with fear.

"Wh-what in the world is going on…?!"

"C-Captain. Shouldn't we withdraw for now…?!"

The ranger and priest cry out in bewilderment.

"This really is strange, Captain… I feel like something's been watching us this entire time. But I can't put my finger on it. I've never felt anything like this before…"

The lancer, with the skill to sense magic over a wide area, can't even sense their opponent.

No one's been injured, but it's reason enough to withdraw.

If this were an ordinary quest, even the captain would consider retreating. But this investigation was a request from the guild.

They can't go back without gathering some information, at the very least. If they leave now, they won't have learned anything.

"…We press on. Lady Emerada said this situation had the potential to evolve into a national disaster. This investigation must be seen through, even if we have to give our lives for it."

"…Huh. So we might die."

"What are you saying? You were prepared for this the moment you signed up as an adventurer."

"I'd hoped to at least make captain one day."

The adventurers nod at one another, preparing themselves for a heroic end, then press on.

With newfound resolve burned into their souls, they begin their do-or-die adventure.

† † †

"Woof. *(You know, I bet those guys are starting to feel pretty bummed over how easy this job is.)*"

"Squeak. *(Probably. Investigating a forest without monsters is just too easy.)*"

"Meow. *(What fortunate adventurers. They'll be able to complete their mission simply by walking.)*"

With the adventurers being protected by Garo and the others, I sprint north with Len on my head and Nahura on my back.

"Arwf... *(Oh, it looks like dawn's almost here...)*"

The sky peeking through the treetops is starting to transition from a dark ultramarine to the light crimson of dawn.

I need to get back to bed before Lady Mary wakes up.

"Woof? *(Let's head back for today. Nahura, if you please?)*"

"Mew! *(Got it. All right then, let's take the anchor off Routa for now and set it to this location. That way, we'll be able to teleport here next time!)*"

Nahura's abilities are so useful.

It's like she has a magical door that can take her anywhere she wants to go.

Nahura meows once, and white space spreads out around us. In the next moment, we're in the mansion's garden.

"Arwf. *(All right, see you later. We'll meet up again tonight.)*"

"Mrow? *(That's fine by me. However, you do know we see each other every mealtime, right?)*"

"Woof! Woof! *(I keep telling you those are* my *meals! Stop eating them like you're entitled to all my food!)*"

Nahura heads for Hecate's workshop, her tail bobbing from side to side.

Damn it. She's definitely going to be picking from my plate all day.

I sigh and head back to my lady's room.

I sneak through the kitchen from the back door, then head down the corridor and up the stairs to the second floor from the main entryway. Finally, I tiptoe to her room in the west wing, using my forepaw to pull down the doorknob and enter as quietly as I can.

My lady is sleeping soundly as always.

"Arwf... *(I'm home...)*"

I wriggle under the duvet.

One problem with this giant canopy bed is that my legs stick out on one end when I lie down. And it's started to creak whenever I climb in.

I need to do something about that, but first, sleep. I'll think about it later.

I continue up through the covers, and my head pops out next to my lady's.

"Hmm… Routa…"

She reaches out subconsciously and hugs me.

"Arww. *(Here I am, my lady.)*"

She hugs me tight, and I'm filled with the joy of being home.

I'll do anything to protect this life. I'll even get those adventurers there and back again safely.

All right then, time to sleep until morning.

I feel a little anxious about the creaking of the bed, but I'm asleep before I know it.

† † †

"Huff…huff… No more…"

The ranger at the head of the party finally falls to his knees.

"Captain… I can't take it anymore… I can't go on…"

It's not just him. The whole party is exhausted.

They're being watched by numerous eyes. But they can't tell where they are. Their observers don't seem to be enemies, but they're certainly not friendly, either. The endless gazes continue chipping away at their sanity.

A whole day has passed since they set foot in the forest, but they haven't had a single battle. There *should* be monsters here, though. The adventurers can sense them. But the moment they get close, the presence of monsters simply vanishes. It always begins when they're struck with the sense that something is about to attack them, but when they reach the place where the monster should be, they find nothing.

That means there's something even more terrifying out there.

Something that even experienced A-Rank adventurers like them can't detect.

It would be less mentally taxing if whatever is out there would just attack them already.

They're all tightly wound, and the tension is wearing away at their nerves.

The eerie gazes are so terrifying that they can't rest comfortably and have no choice but to keep walking.

They've never been on such an arduous journey before.

No matter how they search their memories, none of them can recall ever having a quest as difficult as this one.

"I'm sorry; I just can't..."

The ranger's companions soon join him on the ground one after the other.

They've reached their limit.

"All right, then. We'll set up camp here for the day. Let's take a long break. I'll take first watch. We'll switch in two hours. Sleep as soon as you've finished your meals."

No one says a word about retreating.

The lives of many depend on this mission. A major magical disaster would be catastrophic.

They've resigned themselves to being unable to return without determining the cause. Fleeing isn't an option when they know the severity of the impending disaster will depend on the results of their investigation.

"Ugh, I would kill for some of that meat the dog was eating... It was such a large cut, but it looked so soft..."

"Don't say that... You're going to make us even more miserable... Just pretend this lump of clay is meat..."

"I don't think that's possible......"

Haah, everyone sighs deeply.

"Did the people who made this stuff even try it themselves...?"

"I dunno. I was told they bought it in bulk from the Morgan Trading Co...."

"It's nutritious; I'll give it that. But everything else is...urgh..."

After washing down their nutritional yet nasty provisions with lukewarm water, the men sleep like logs.

† † †

"Arwf. *(All right, let's head back out now that our bellies are full.)*"

"Squea. *(It has been one full day. They've probably traveled quite a distance already.)*"

"Mrow. *(Their mission will be complete soon enough, and then they can go home.)*"

We meet in the garden again in the dead of night.

We polish off the light midnight snack that I brought, and Nahura teleports us with her magic.

My field of vision is filled with white light, and not even a second later, the scenery changes to the nighttime forest.

Yellow eyes are waiting for us.

"Grwl. *(My king. I am glad to see you have returned safely.)*"

It's the pitch-black Fen Wolf, Garo.

Her fur's so black, I can barely make her out in the dark forest.

For a moment, I think she's a ghost, and I almost scream, but that'll be our little secret.

"W-woof. *(W-well, if it isn't Garo. I'm surprised you knew where we'd be.)*"

"Grwl. *(I followed your scent until it vanished here, so I knew we would meet again if I waited.)*"

Of course. What amazing tracking skills wolves have.

But it's also stalker-ish and a little scary.

"Woof? *(Where are the adventurers now? They must have traveled quite a ways without getting into any fights.)*"

I immediately ask Garo for an update.

But her reply is less than ideal.

"Arwf?! *(What?! No way, they've barely progressed at all?!)*"

"Grwl. *(Yes. I don't know why, but they were incredibly exhausted.*

They have set up camp much farther to the south from here. At this rate, it will be some time before they reach the waterfall.)"

So they haven't even passed this point yet.

"Woof. *(Hmm, the forest is a cruel mistress. I honestly thought they'd breeze through it, since they're adventurers and all.)*"

Could it be they're low-ranking adventurers?

We'll have to protect them even more now.

"Woof. *(Well, I guess it works out better if they're slow. It'll take a while to get things ready. We three will continue to the waterfall. Garo, you and the others continue to guard them. And double your efforts.)*"

"Grwl! *(As you command, my king! Just leave it to us!)*"

I watch Garo bolt upright when suddenly, something bugs me.

"Woof? *(Hey, Garo? Have you gotten smaller?)*"

I was sure Garo was larger than me.

But now she's not.

"Grwl. *(With all due respect, my king. I have not gotten smaller. It is you who has grown.)*"

I understand what she's saying.

"Woof. *(Oh, right. It's still only been two months since I was born. Of course I'd still be growing.)*"

When I think about it, I do now have to squeeze my body through the back door, and the bed keeps creaking whenever I'm in it.

Looks like I've grown even bigger without realizing it.

Wait a minute. That's a huge problem…

"G-grwl… *(U-um, you're not just bigger, but stronger, too! Much more magnificent…)*"

Ugh, please don't look all bashful while saying things like that.

It doesn't make my heart flutter or anything. I'm *not* a furry.

"Captain…! The gazes have become more intense than yesterday…!"

"I—I think their numbers have also increased…!"

"F-foul beasts! Where are you?! Show yourself! Come out right now…!"

"What is this forest?!?!"

The more-intense gazes leave the adventurers in shock.

They begin to doubt they'll reach their destination safely.

Fear and anxiety weigh down on them as the heroic A-Rank adventurers take another step deep into the forest.

† † †

"Snork…pheew…snork…pheew…"

The next morning, I'm asleep at the bottom of the stairs in the entranceway, my legs acting as a pillow, crossed under my head.

The cold marble floor feels fantastic on hot days.

When I sleep here, anyone who passes by gives me attention, so it's a pretty good spot.

Lying here and dozing off all day is another one of my pleasures.

"…You asleep?"

Is that timid voice Zenobia's?

I sneak a peek and see Zenobia looking left and right, making sure no one's around.

"…………"

Slowly, she reaches a hand out and touches my head.

I don't sense any desire to kill, but there is a tiny bit of fear as her hand starts to gently caress my fur.

"Tch…this is…really…"

Looks like Zenobia's become a slave to the fluff.

Her hand moves from my head down to my flank, innocently petting my soft fur.

Oh, Zenobia, you're really not honest with yourself. You can pet me anytime.

"Heh-heh-heh…"

Her face scrunches up as she breaks out into a smile.

Dishonest Zenobia is so cute. I really wanna lick her.

If I wake up now, I bet she'll make a great face, but I'm scared she'll get mad instead.

I'll continue pretending to sleep.

Actually, I really am sleepy. I could fall asleep just like this.

I get sleepy when people pet me. It's just another thing I've learned about myself since becoming a dog.

Then I hear footsteps coming from the second floor. Those light footsteps belong to Lady Mary.

"Urk...!"

Zenobia's shoulders freeze in surprise, and she quickly stands up and leaves.

Boy oh boy, she really needs to be more honest with herself.

Well, she'd never willingly show anyone that side of her anyway. But something tells me I'll get to see it again.

Hee-hee-hee. She's slowly becoming more affectionate toward me. She's stopped trying to kill me, too.

"Routa, Routa, what are you doing? Are you tired? Should we cancel our lunch playtime?"

"Arww. *(Oh, sorry. I was off in the clouds.)*"

My lady's sweet voice calls me back from dreamland.

I look up to see her lovely blue eyes. She's beautiful today as well.

If Lady Mary is here, then that means she's all done with her morning studies.

Mmm, I don't feel like I've slept at all. Every evening, I've been so focused on helping the adventurers that I haven't really gotten a chance to rest.

"Yaaaaaaaawn......"

I let out a big yawn.

"Hee-hee, oh, Routa."

Lady Mary giggles.

She's so cute. What an angel.

"Arwf. *(Just give me a minute.)*"

I'm incredibly tired, but it's time to rise.

This lazy hound doesn't want to work at all, but I'll do anything for the sake of my lady's happiness.

"Arwf. *(Up we get.)*"

I manage to stand up, but my eyelids are so heavy, I can't seem to open them.

Ugh, I really shouldn't have done several all-nighters in a row...

When are the adventurers going to reach the waterfall? If they don't get there soon, they'll be wasting my hospitality.

I told Garo that the Fen Wolves needed to double their efforts. I wonder if I should have the whole pack follow the adventurers.

The image of the adventurers screaming "Please! Have mercy!" pops into the back of my mind, but it probably doesn't mean anything.

"Thanks, Routa. Don't push yourself, though. Let's read a book under the tree. I'll go get something to read and meet you there."

With that, Lady Mary runs up the stairs.

"Arwf! *(Take your time, my lady!)*"

I made her worry about me. What disgraceful, improper behavior for a pet.

At the same time, I'm not opposed to her showering me with kindness.

My half-lidded eyes are still bleary as I leave the entranceway and head to the garden.

There is a splendid tree growing right in the center of the garden. I plop down beneath it.

The area's gotten hotter with the midday sun, but the treetops block out the sun nicely. And the breeze that sets the leaves rustling feels delightful.

The breeze carries the scent of flowers, and the sun leaking through the leaves makes me sleepy.

Oh no. This is bad. It's too easy to slip into laziness.

This is a way better napping spot than the marble floor.

This space feels so good, I'm going to fall asleep again.

"Squee... *(Hnya, hmm... Tee-hee, flattery will get you nowhere, my darling...)*"

Here I am, trying not to pass out, and I look over to see my free-loader talking in her sleep.

Damn it, Len, how dare you sleep so soundly on someone else's back.

I'm pretty sure she sleeps and eats more than anyone else.

"Were you waiting long?"

As I fight my resentment and sleepiness, my lady suddenly arrives with a book in hand.

The thin scarf draped over her shoulders is super-cute.

"Woof, woof. *(Not at all; I just got here.)*"

"Hee-hee, it feels like a rendezvous."

"Woof, woof. *(Yeah. It's like a date. Hee-hee.)*"

As she holds the book behind her back with a bashful look on her face, I'm reminded that Lady Mary is truly the cutest girl in the whole wide world.

Looks like her hair fluttering in the breeze is poking her nose. I want to sniff it.

"Excuse me."

"Arwf. *(Of course, have a seat.)*"

My lady sits down on the lawn, leaning against me as I sprawl out on the ground.

My fluffy body engulfs her petite frame.

"I brought a book of fairy tales with me today. The man I named you after is in here, too."

"Arwf. *(Oooh.)*"

Wasn't he some legendary hero who saved the world a long time ago? I remember seeing a stone statue of him in the Royal Capital.

We have the same name, but we're nothing alike. I couldn't put my life on the line to fight for the world.

That's basically working 24-7.

Ugh, no thank you. That would be just as bad as working at that terrible company from my old world.

But I shouldn't complain about the name my lady gave me.

Then again, my name was Routa in the other world, too.

Legendary hero Routa, this good-for-nothing dog Routa will live a self-indulgent life of eating and sleeping just for you. Don't worry, though—you'll still be the one kids look up to.

"He was an incredibly strong, incredibly brave, and incredibly kind person. Just like you, Routa!"

"Woof, woof! *(Aw, really? You're making me blush!)*"

He's completely different from me, but I'm happy my lady is complimenting me anyway.

"Squeak! *(Enough of this farce! Have some pride! Don't act so bashful over some human girl!)*"

"Arwf! *(Ah! Hey!)*"

Len had woken up at some point and climbed up my neck, and she's now standing on my head.

"Arwf! *(I told you not to come out!)*"

I haven't told anyone at the mansion about you! I'm waiting for the right time to say you're Hecate's familiar. They're way more likely to believe that than the alternative.

Do you even know what you look like? A mouse! A *mouse*! The most reviled pest ever. The kind that carries horrible diseases.

I thought it would be fine because you normally hide, but then you jump out now!

"Oh!"

Lady Mary sees the arrogant blue mouse on my head and cries out in surprise.

I'm sorry, my lady!

Please spare her life!

"How cute!"

......Oh, that's actually a good reaction.

But still, *cute*?

You think a rodent who has a bad biting habit is *cute*...?!

I won't forgive you for calling someone who's not me cute. I can feel the jealousy welling up.

"A-arwf! *(I'm cuter than this tiny thing! Lady Mary, look at me! I'm cute! Isn't my tail wagging cute?!)*"

"Squee… *(There can be no comparison…)*"

Shut it, you.

What will be left for me if you steal my position as family pet?

All I'll have left is the stigma that comes with being a monster, a creature to be exterminated! Lady Mary's number one pet has to be me!

"Are you Routa's friend?"

It doesn't matter who my lady is talking to—her attitude never changes. Even with a pipsqueak like this. Her eyes lock with Len's, and she gives her the proper greetings.

"Hello there. I am Meariya Von Faulks."

"Squeak. *(Hmm, I give you credit for your admirable behavior. I am the blue dragon Lenowyrm.)*"

Hey, you told her your name, but she can't understand you.

All she can see is a mouse squeaking at her.

"It's a pleasure to meet you, cute little mouse."

"Squee. *(H-hey. Don't pet my head.)*"

Len protests as my lady tickles her head with her fingertips.

But it doesn't take long.

Len soon falls for Lady Mary's finger technique, melting on her belly until she resembles a soft rice cake.

"Right here? Does that feel good?"

"S-squee. *(Sh-shtaaap… D-don't touch meeee…… Or dooooooo…)*"

I watch Lady Mary and Len enjoying themselves, and I internally bite on a handkerchief in frustration.

G-grrrrrrrr! N-not faaaaaiiiir!

First Nahura, and now even Len has stolen my lady's heart.

Damn it! Damn it!

The only one she should pet is me!

I'm going crazy with jealousy.

Come *oooon*, Lady Mary! Pay attention to me, too! Look at me!

"Hee-hee. Okay, everyone, let's read."

She doesn't register my jealousy as she places Len on her shoulder and opens the hardcover book.

I figured it was just a hardback novel, but the inside looks like a nursery book with illustrations.

I wonder if she picked something simple because she is going to read to me.

My lady, you're far too kind. I want to serve you for the rest of my life.

"Once upon a time, the world was on the brink of ruin thanks to an evil Demon Lord. The Demon Lord was strong and trampled the weak like straw."

"Squeak. *(Hmph. How strong can one Demon Lord be? I'm sure I'm much stronger.)*"

"But despite the Demon Lord's fearsome strength, he had five attendees known as the Five Demon Generals."

The Five Demon Generals is a pretty nerdy name, but my lady continues.

The ruler of the dead who led evil spirits, Lich.

The demon-conquering ambassador of Hell, Belgor.

The demonic ruler of one hundred terrible beasts, Behemoth.

The pure-blooded immortal vampire princess, Carmila.

The commander of ancient giants, Gigas.

"These generals brought together the five species that decimated human lands one after another."

"Squeak. *(Hmph, I don't know of an era when the dragons were ruled over. Anyone who tried that would quickly find the tables turned on them.)*"

This spinster is trying to get one up on everything my lady is reading.

That's really lame, Miss Spinster. You sound like some punk from the boonies, Miss Spinster. You're past your prime, Miss Spinster.

"Then came a young man who stood for the people. He gathered the soldiers of fallen countries and met the Demon Lord's army face-to-face."

Her thin white fingers turn the page.

"His name was Routa. With his legendary sword, he defeated one of the Five Demon Generals, then another, and another."

"Squeak. *(Oh, not bad. It doesn't sound like he was a pervert, either, so he's probably better than you, my darling.)*"

"Bark, bark! *(He was probably a pervert, too! I mean—I'm not a pervert! I'm a dog! I'm a dog; it's only natural!)*"

There's nothing weird about dogs licking and sniffing people.

If I were a human, I would be thrown in prison right away, right? But I'm a dog, so it's fine.

Being a dog is great. I want to stay a dog and be fussed over and petted.

"Squeak. *(You're giving off an unsavory aura, my darling. Besides, you're not a dog; you're the king of the Fen Wolves.)*"

"Bark! *(I'm a dog! One hundred percent dog!)*"

It's just that my body's a little big, my face is scary, and when I howl, I fire a beam of light that feels like I'm throwing up.

But no matter what, I'm still a dog. Because I want to live as this mansion's pet for all eternity.

I want everyone to fuss over me and pet me as I eat too much and sleep a ton.

That's right. I shall live the lazy life the brave man with my name would have wanted!

Looks like my lady's reading is coming to a close as I argue with Len.

"And so, the hero Routa defeated the Demon Lord, saving the world and living happily ever after with the princess of his hometown."

How clichéd.

Ptooie.

Popular guys are my natural enemy.

"Squee. *(Are you not popular, my darling? At the very least, you have me, your beautiful princess, by your side.)*"

"Woof, woof. *(You're a mouse, you know. And even if you transform, you're still a dragon. You could at least* try *to look human.)*"

"Squeak. *(…Hee-hee, patience, my darling. I'll grant that wish someday.)*"

"W-woof? *(Wh-what…?)*"

Len huffs through her nose triumphantly but doesn't explain further.

"Miss? Lunch is ready."

The twin-tailed Toa arrives with news that lunch is ready.

Our eyes meet for a split second, but she immediately looks away.

Oh, right. You're working. This puppy feels lonely now.

"Thank you, Toa. I'll head right in."

My lady closes her book, stands up, and straightens out her dress.

"Routa, little mouse. Let's play again later once I've finished my lunch."

"Woof! *(Okay! I'll be waiting!)*"

"Squee! *(Very well. You are admirable, for a human. But* I *am my darling's wife! Don't you forget it!)*"

You're not. Stop saying that.

My lady looks adorable as she waves her good-bye, and behind her, Toa gives a little wave, too.

As I watch them go, I'm overcome with a warm, fuzzy feeling.

Then Len bites me. It really hurts.

† † †

The happy scene occurring at the mansion far away means nothing to the adventurers whose minds and bodies are being pushed to the limit.

The four men sit in a circle around the small firepit, restlessly chewing on their provisions.

Though they are a good source of nutrition, nothing can erase the strong plantlike flavor weaved into the claylike texture.

These unpleasant rations—their only food—further chip away at their sanity.

Deep in the forest where no light reaches, they cannot tell if it is night or day.

Without even a single birdsong, the silence in the forest is unsettling.

They cannot even sense animals passing by.

And all around them, the eyes are watching, accompanied by the occasional menacing feel like one set of eyes is about to attack.

The shapeless creatures do not rest, and they watch the adventurers even now.

"......This is hell......"

It's not clear who mumbles that.

No one replies.

What's the point in repeating the obvious?

There is no light in their eyes. Their cheeks are hollow. Their hair is disheveled, but there's no point in fixing it.

Their mental fatigue is impacting their bodies.

No longer do they appear as skilled adventurers, but rather, pitiful victims.

"..........."

The captain with the claymore on his back sluggishly rises to his feet.

The party says nothing as they extinguish the fire and collect their things.

They haven't slept. They're too afraid to sleep anymore.

How could the mysterious creatures watching them really wear them down this much?

The adventurers march onward, their legs dragging like they are full of lead.

They walk, just walk, like lost souls.

† † †

"Woof. *(Hmm, this is bad.)*"

I mumble as I look down at the scene below the hill.

Garo led me here to observe the adventurers dragging their feet as they walk.

They all look so hollow, it's as if all thoughts besides walking have vanished.

What terrible exhaustion.

This sparks a memory. I've felt that way before in the other world.

They have such a strong escort guarding them. Why are they this tired?

"Mrow… *(It's probably* that*…)*"

"Squeak. *(Hmm, I think so, too. It has to be.)*"

Len and Nahura nod in agreement.

"Woof. *(You two noticed it, too? I've been wondering if that was the problem.)*"

Our goal is to give the adventurers a safe journey.

But even though they already have such a great guard, they don't look happy at all.

It's like they're walking through hell.

There's only one reason they'd feel this way.

"Woof! / Mrow! / Squeak! *(They need a bigger escort!)*"

We say our conclusions aloud.

"Grwl! *(So that* was *it!)*"

Garo thought so, too? She seems relieved to hear it.

"Grwl. *(I never expected the humans to be this weak. I shall gather every remaining Fen Wolf I can.)*"

Garo directs Bal and the other wolves standing behind her. The Fen Wolves immediately split off into four directions to summon reinforcements.

"Woof. *(Yes, good. The adventurers* must *have a safe journey.)*"

"Meow. *(Hee-hee, it feels nice to do a good deed.)*"

"Squeak. *(I feel like we may be spoiling them. However, I suppose we must if we are to protect our way of life at the mansion. We'll escort them to the ends of the earth.)*"

We all nod in satisfaction.

"Grwl! *(Just leave it to us, my king. In the name of the Fen Wolves, not even a single ant shall get through our defenses!)*"

""""Grwl! Grwl! Grwl! *(King! King! King!)*""""

The Fen Wolves are riled up. Now I'm *sure* the adventurers will be able to reach their destination in peace.

06 I'm Helping! ...Or So I Thought, but I Was Wrong *Again*!

"Woof! *(All right! We're here!)*"

We break out of the thicket, and the moonlight shines down on us.

We've finally arrived at our destination. We are able to exit the forest ahead of the adventurers.

Below us is a stream flowing through a wide riverbed.

It'll probably take the adventurers another two to three days to get here.

Plenty of time to prepare.

"Squee? *(Darling, what in the world do you plan to do here? The remains of our battle are off in that direction.)*"

Exactly as she says, the cave we fought in is a little farther north from here.

However, that's not where I want to execute my plan.

"Mewl. *(Hmm. You mentioned you wanted to give the adventurers a treat, but you haven't yet told us what that treat is.)*"

"Woof. *(I'm going to prepare it right now. You're going to help, too.)*"

I survey the area for a suitable location.

Somewhere close to the river but not too close. About twenty meters away should do. This place with a bunch of round stones polished by the river should be perfect.

"Woof… *(Well, it's been a while, but…)*"

I open my mouth a little and howl.

Magic coalesces in my mouth, and a narrow beam fires. I aim just in front of my feet, firing the beam of light straight down, piercing right through stone, dirt, and bedrock.

"Squee? *(…What are you doing, my darling?)*"

"Mewl? *(Are you looking for earthworms to eat? They're not very tasty, you know.)*"

That's not it.

I'm not going to eat anything.

Wait, Nahura's tried earthworms?

"Woof? *(All right, you see the mountains near here?)*"

We look up over the waterfall and toward what people called the sacred mountains.

"Woof. *(If you dig deep enough in an area like this, a hot spring will pop up… Maybe.)*"

And with that, I point my snout down in the same place and blast my vomit beam.

I try howling for longer so it will reach deeper.

The beam continues on for as long as I continue to howl. I'm able to dig really deep down.

Apparently, the intensity of my howl *does* change the beam's power, and the length of time I howl for changes the range.

I'm really getting the hang of how to use this beam. The key is to feel like you're vomiting when you fire it. I have to be careful; if I'm not careful, then I actually *will* throw up.

"Squeak. *(The more I watch you, the more I am convinced that's a messy way to control that power. Then again, it is extremely powerful destructive magic you're firing.)*"

"Woof? *(What? So you can't do this?)*"

"Squeak! *(D-don't be ridiculous! I am a dragon. There is magic in this world that I can and cannot control. Extremely destructive magic is easy. But I am not proficient in regulation. It's strange that you can fire it like that.)*"

"Woof. *(Oh, I get it. You're a sore loser.)*"

"Squeak! *(I am not!)*"

Just then, I hear a bubbling coming from the hole I just dug.

"Woof! *(Oh, it's here!)*"

"Squea? *(What's here?)*"

"Mewl? *(That thing you called a hot spring?)*"

Len and Nahura peek into the hole.

"Woof! *(Ah, don't, you idiots—!)*"

The bubbling sound turns into a low rumble, and a second later, water bursts out of the hole.

"Squeeeeeeee?! *(Wh-whaaaaaaaaat?!)*"

"Meeeooowww?! *(E-eeeeeeeeek?!)*"

Len and Nahura are thrown into the air by the waterspout.

They're not ordinary animals, so I'm not too worried about them, but I run over to the direction they're thrown in, catching Len in my mouth and Nahura on my back.

"Mew… *(Ahh…)*"

"Squee… *(I'm dizzy…)*"

A moment later, spring water falls on us like rain.

"Woof! *(That's hot! —Or not…)*"

It's the perfect tepid temperature.

Just because it's spring water doesn't mean it's going to be boiling hot.

This is great. I had anticipated the hot-spring water mixing with the river water to cool down, so this works out perfectly.

"Woof? *(Nahura! Can you cover the hole with a large boulder for me?)*"

"M-mewl. *(S-sure. Just leave it to me.)*"

I look around to see that Nahura has gotten up and buried herself beneath my belly.

She pops her face out from between my legs and floats a boulder buried in the river with her magic.

"Woof? *(…Why are you between my legs?)*"

"Mewl. *(You're a good rain shield. I absolutely* hate *getting wet.)*"

Oh yeah, she hates baths, too.

I'll have to force her into the hot spring when it's done.

She's starting to smell. Like a damp cloth.

"Mewl? *(How's that?)*"

She rests the boulder on top of the hole, and the rush of warm water stops.

"Woof. *(It's great.)*"

I use my large beam to open two holes on either side of the boulder. The beam doesn't crack the stone at all and instead creates two tunnels.

I then jump on top of the boulder and fire a narrower beam than the one before straight down through it.

This hole overlaps perfectly with the hot-spring hole I opened before.

Of course, this means the warm water comes pouring out in three directions.

The left and right holes are bigger, so the water doesn't shoot out, but the one in the center sprays up into the air with the same energy as before.

"Woof? *(Hey, Nahura, can you cover this hole up now? The one in the middle.)*"

"Mewl. *(Sure, sure. I guess Hecate isn't the only one who likes to push around cat familiars.)*"

Nahura remains under me as she stuffs in a rock that's roughly the size of the hole with her magic.

This causes the water that was welling out of the top to split left and right.

The water flow isn't too strong and flows in an arc onto the ground.

"Bark. *(All right, now can you cover the left and right holes.)*"

Nahura covers the holes with rocks just as before.

"Squee. *(Hmm. I have no idea what you're trying to do, darling.)*"

"Bark. *(You'll see.)*"

I begin to fiercely dig around the boulder.

"Woof. *(There. That'll do.)*"

I've dug a donut ring into the riverbed around the boulder.

It's only about fifty centimeters deep but is quite wide, giving me a lot of space.

"Bark. *(Right, then. Please open the left and right holes.)*"

"Mewl. *(Okaaaay.)*"

The stones plop out, and the water flows freely again. It slowly fills up the donut-shaped hole I dug.

There's still soil left in the hole, which quickly turns the water brown, but that's fine for now.

"Bark. *(That should be full enough. Please plug them again.)*"

The water stops, leaving us with a spring that's an ordinary brown color.

"Woof. *(We'll leave it for today and come back tomorrow when the soil's settled.)*"

"Mrow! *(Okay, I'll set the anchor here, and we can head back!)*"

"Squee. *(I still have no idea what you're trying to do, beloved.)*"

Len tilts her head, and we teleport back to the mansion with Nahura, who has no idea what the future holds for her.

I wash the mud off my body in the garden's fountain and shake the water off with all my might.

Then I slip back into bed with Lady Mary, looking completely innocent.

"Hmm......Routa......?"

"Arww. *(Yes, I'm here.)*"

Phew, that was a close one. But today was another successful "mission complete."

My lady subconsciously hugs me, and I'm reminded of her softness as I soon fall asleep.

† † †

"Mmm, you're so warm, Routa."

She wraps her arms around my body, enjoying my coat.

"Arwf! *(Oh, Lady Mary! You're so bold.)*"

"Mmm, so fluffy."

Hee-hee, the fur around my cheek is particularly soft, right? You can pet me more if you'd like.

She buries her face into my white fur and breathes deep, drowning me in affection.

I would not lay a paw on such a beauty. But it doesn't count if she's the one who touches me.

As she lies on my belly and rocks her body back and forth, I spot a maid in traditional attire.

It's Miranda. She's as neat, tidy, and cute as always.

"It's time to get up, miss."

She has approached silently and now calls out to Lady Mary.

"...Aw, time flies when you're having fun."

She rubs her face into my chest in protest.

"Very well, my lady. I shall return a little later."

"But then you'll be scolded, Miranda. Sorry for being so selfish. I'll get up."

Lady Mary is such a good girl. She always puts others before herself.

This no-good mutt sometimes worries that she doesn't take care of herself because of it.

I'm sure that when we ran away to the lake a while ago, it was because of all the stress that had built up. I need to offer her my glossy, fluffy body for further therapy. As her beloved pet, I want to help my lady de-stress. I'll never surrender this sovereign duty to Nahura or Len.

Jealousy burns in me for all the small creatures that have stolen my lady's heart from me.

"Routa, we'll play again later."

She seems reluctant to leave as she gets up.

"Woof, woof! *(Let me know if you ever you want to skip your studies! You can hop on my back, and we'll run away!)*"

Although, I'll come back as soon as I'm hungry. Then we can get scolded together.

I can be brave for my lady even if we get scolded! I don't care if she develops a tiny delinquent streak!

"Squeak... *(I know you just want to play, but you always get so bashful around that girl......)*"

Ever since Len experienced the petting prowess of Lady Mary, she's hidden herself deep in my fur and doesn't come out whenever my lady is around.

She said something about not wanting anyone to touch her except for her husband, even if it's another female.

"Woof? *(What's thiiiis? Len, are you jealous?)*"

"Squeak! *(Yes, I am! So pay attention! Pay attention to me more!)*"

"Woof! *(Wow! So honest! And ouch! That hurts!)*"

Stop biting me whenever you can't think of a comeback.

I guess I am the one who destroyed her last home, but now that she's taken up residence in my fur, she steals my food and bites me when she gets irrationally jealous. I'm at my wit's end.

I see Miranda leave the mansion with the shift change, and Toa starts to work.

She's working hard again today.

She's carrying the heavy laundry basket as usual. I can see it piled up with white sheets.

She finally gets to the long clothesline and tries as hard as always to stand on her tiptoes and hang up the sheets.

But it doesn't look like it's going well. It would help if she had a footstool or something.

"Arwf. *(Oh, right, I just remembered.)*"

I run over to Toa.

"Woof! Woof! *(Toa! Toa!)*"

"Eek!"

Oh, whoops. I forgot that barking like that scares the crap out of her.

I thought we had gotten closer since the incident the other day, but it looks like I made her cry again.

"..........."

Toa, whose shoulders are frozen in surprise, turns around.

"...What is it, Routa?"

Oh, she's not scared?

No, now that I take a closer look, I can see she's trembling, but she hasn't gone into a panic like before. She's being careful not to hurt my feelings.

G-great. So let's take advantage of this newfound bravery by letting me help you.

I go right up to her and lie on my belly.

"Huh? Routa?"

She tilts her head in confusion, not understanding what I'm trying to suggest.

She stares right at me lying prone.

I don't know if it's the way her maid clothes move at this angle, or if her skirt is just short, but when I tilt my head at just the right angle, I can see right up— No, that's bad!

Shut up, brain!

"Arww. *(Come on, Toa. Climb up.)*"

If you don't have a footstool, then you can use me instead!

"...Do you want me to get on?"

"Woof! *(Yes! By Jove, I think she's got it!)*"

"You want to help me? But..."

Nooo, no buts.

I paw at her.

"Fine... Thank you."

She giggles and takes off her shoes.

"Is that okay? I'm not too heavy, am I?"

"Arwf... *(Oh-ho, this is quite...)*"

The feeling of her soft stockings and light body seems to have awoken a new pleasure in me.

I feel like I'm starting to understand how Christina feels.

"Squee? *(What an unsightly expression... Isn't this one even more of a child than the last female...?)*"

That's not it. Don't say something so rude about Toa.

It's fine! I'm not doing anything wrong! Different worlds have different rules!

With me as her footstool, Toa gets the laundry on the line in no time.

"Thanks, Routa."

"Arwf. *(No problem at all. Thank* you.*)*"

I don't know if I should say *you're welcome* or *thank you.*

"I'm sorry for getting scared that time. You haven't changed at all from when you were a pup."

No, I'm sorry I scared you.

Now that I think about it, I *do* look scary. But I believe that if I can help out like this, then Toa'll think I'm cute like she used to.

She gives me a little wave, picks up the empty laundry basket, and heads back to the mansion.

"*Yaaaaaaaawn… (One job, and I'm already exhausted…)*"

Sooo sleepy. I should take a nap so I'm not tired tonight.

Tonight's the night we finish it!

† † †

"Woof, woof. *(That's it, you need to lay the entire thing with stones. Slowly now. If you rush it, you'll kick up the settled dirt.)*"

"Meow. *(Okay, leave it to me.)*"

Bathed in moonlight, Nahura gets to work with her levitation powers.

With a flick of her paw, stones from the river float up and one by one sink to the bottom of the spring.

The stones have been smoothed round by the river, making them a great floor to sit on when laid out correctly.

The once-warm water in the donut-shaped hole is now freezing, but it's also beautifully clear after being left alone for a day.

The stones cover the dirt carefully so as not to move the water too much.

Nahura's magic really is useful. We can do this without much labor or any heavy machinery.

"Mrow? *(How does that look?)*"

Stones of various sizes lie on one another so there are no gaps. The dirt shouldn't get kicked up into the water now.

"Bark, bark! *(Great! Next is the waterway.)*"

I leap over the spring onto the riverside.

I stick the tip of my nose under the water at an angle so there'll be a slight slope.

"Blurbl! *(Little beam!)*"

A hole opens from the spring to the river in a flash, causing the water on the edge to cascade out into the river.

A perfect free-flowing hot spring.

The ever-circulating spring will help maintain the temperature, and the overflowing water will be fed back into the river.

"Woof! *(Open the gate! Opeeeen!)*"

"Mewl. *(All right, all right.)*"

With a *pop, pop,* Nahura removes the plugs from the boulder in the middle of the spring, and hot water flows out of the left and right sides.

The arcs of spring water are quite impressive, and now the colder water will soon warm up.

"Awoooo! *(All right, then! It's done!)*"

"Mewl! *(Congratulations!)*"

Nahura gives me soundless applause as I howl with joy.

"Squeak? *(So? What is it?)*"

Len questions me, stomping on my head.

She's acting pretty haughty, but she never lifted a paw to help.

"Squea? *(It resembles the water fountain back at the mansion… What's the point of it?)*"

"Arwf?! *(Huh?! You still don't know?!)*"

You've gotta be kidding me.

"Mewl. *(I don't know, either.)*"

Yeah, I guess it's fine if you don't understand. It would honestly make things harder if you did.

It's best that you don't know until you try it yourself.

"Grwl! *(My king! I have a report!)*"

Garo and a few other Fen Wolves come up to me just as we complete the hot spring.

"Grwl. *(The adventurers will be here soon.)*"

"Woof? *(Ah, they finally made it?)*"

"Grwl. *(Not a single one of them has been harmed. We eliminated all monsters on the way.)*"

"Woof. *(Oh, nice work.)*"

"Grwl! *(I-it is an honor to be praised by you!)*"

Garo and the other wolves are so moved they lie on their bellies and tremble.

They're always so weird about proving their loyalty.

But since Garo and the other wolves don't want to be equals, I'll have to reward them for their efforts.

A job well done should be rewarded, after all.

I am just barely able to see my plan through to the end before the adventurers get here.

Thanks to the Fen Wolves' thorough escort duties, the adventurers are able to have a relaxing trip.

But despite the lack of danger and injuries, walking all the time must still be tiring.

There's where the hot spring comes in.

There's nothing better than soaking your tired body in warm water, and eating delicious food should energize their bodies a hundred times over. Their long journey is over, and they can go home feeling refreshed and accomplished.

That's why I made this plan, "Hot-Spring Vacation! Drip, Drop!"

Huh? What's going *drip, drop*, you ask?

Well, that would be the adventurer's— You know what? Never mind.

"Woof! *(Nahura! Bring out the food we collected.)*"

"Mewl! *(Okay!)*"

She activates her teleportation magic.

The basket with little bits of bread, ham, and cheese that I had snuck out of the kitchen at night falls out of her magic circle.

The poor adventurers, who have been eating nothing but those disgusting-looking rations, should have a feast with this.

They're preserved foods, but old man James made them. Which means they'll taste heavenly.

I'm sure they'll be satisfied.

I place the basket next to the hot spring, and now everything is ready.

Now all that's missing are the guests of honor.

"Woof! *(Okay, everyone, hide in the shadows and watch over them!)*"

The Fen Wolves disperse, hiding themselves in the shadow of a boulder or the long grass.

"Arwf, arwf? *(Are they here yet? Are they here yet?)*"

"Nom, nom. *(They won't arrive immediately. Have some patience.)*"

"Nibble, nibble, nibble. *(Yes, that's right. Haste makes waste, you know.)*"

"Woof! Woof?! *(Hey, what are you two eating?!)*"

They're both holding food from the basket.

"Mrow. *(It's just a taste. Just a taste.)*"

"Squee. *(That's right. I need to check for poison. You should thank me.)*"

"Bark, bark! *(No fair! Let me have some!)*"

"Grwl… *(M-my king. Please be silent…)*"

I hear human footsteps coming from the forest as we argue like always.

"Woof! *(They're here! Silence everyone.* Munch, munch.*)*"

"Squeak… *(You're the loudest one here, darling. And I won't forgive you for stealing my cheese…)*"

"Meow… *(He took my sausage, too……)*"

I only took a little!

Don't act like I took everything!

I can slowly see the outline of humans coming from deep in the forest.

"Uwah…"

"Urgh…"

The four adventurers emerge from the forest looking absolutely ghastly.

They haven't been fighting, so their equipment isn't torn. Only their boots are covered in mud. But they still look like death.

Even zombies have healthier-looking faces than these guys.

I'm not entirely sure if they're conscious. They look worse than I did when I died of overwork with a zillion bags under my eyes.

"Squee? *(Hey, why do they look so tired? All they did was walk, right?)*"

"Mewl. *(Yeah, maybe it's because they're such low-ranking adventurers.)*"

"Squee. *(Honestly, humans are so weak.)*"

"Woof. *(Oh well. It'll all be worth it once they start relaxing.)*"

They should have learned along the way that the forest is completely safe.

Now they just have to relax in the hot spring and stuff themselves.

I hold my breath, waiting for the adventurers to see the treat before them.

† † †

"Uwah…"

"Urgh…"

The death march comes to an end as the adventurers break free of the deep forest. Before them lies the dried riverbed, bathed in moonlight.

Even though the moon is half-hidden by clouds, the pale light is almost blinding to their eyes, which have become used to the darkness.

Having been through the wringer, the weathered adventurers finally feel their sanity returning.

"...Where is the destination point...?" the captain with the claymore asks the ranger.

"...Just a little farther. We should reach it by sunrise at this rate...," spits the ranger, exhausted and with drool hanging from his mouth.

The instrument the guild loaned him is reacting very strongly. Their destination must be incredibly close.

The captain glances behind them.

The fatigued priest and steely lancer at the rear have become little more than groaning mannequins.

Their exhaustion is incredibly bad. They don't know what's going to happen at the investigation point, either.

It's too dangerous to go on like this.

"...We should rest here while we can. We're in no shape to conduct the investigation..."

The mysterious eyes that were following them until this point have gone away.

They should be able to rest for a little while now.

They have no idea what the creatures wanted with them. Maybe they were simply hoping to torment them? They never did get to see what the creatures looked like in the end.

"We don't need a lookout... There's no point... Just rest for as long as you like..."

If the creatures were going to kill them, they would have attacked them ages ago. And even if they were attacked, the group no longer has the stamina to fight back.

Recovering strength and energy is their top priority. Even if only a little, they need to be as refreshed as possible before moving on to conduct their investigation.

The whole party collapses by the riverbank. They throw down their things, sit on the ground, and let out sighs of exhaustion.

It's incredibly improper behavior for A-Rank adventurers, but there's no one around to point that out.

"Captain... What do you suppose that is...?"

The first one to notice the anomaly is the ranger.

Steam can be seen rising just a short distance from them.

"What is that...?"

It's hard to get back up again after they just caught a break, but they have to check it out.

The captain heads over to the steam with the rest of the party following behind.

"What in the world...?"

It's a circular stream. It looks man-made. There's no way something like this occurred naturally.

The ranger takes off his glove and dips his hand into the water.

"It's warm. There's also a faint smell of sulfur. It's a hot spring."

"Out here?"

In the middle of the hot spring is a giant boulder, with plenty of warm water flowing out of the central hole.

He's seen a lot of naturally forming hot springs before. But someone clearly made this one.

"Do you think anyone lives near here?"

"Impossible. I heard this forest is unexplored. The reason we're even here is because no one lives near where that magical disaster occurred."

"Then what *is* this?"

"If you think about it, maybe the things that were watching us this whole time made it?"

"Then our situation really is hopeless..."

This completely changes what they thought about their stalkers simply being strong monsters.

The carefully placed stones. The boulder carved to provide hot water. Now that they look closer, there's even a waterway dug out to the river to let out cooled water.

This means there are creatures intelligent enough to make something like this deep in the forest.

It wouldn't just be hopeless, but the worst of the worst situations imaginable.

"C-Captain. Do you see that…?"

The lancer is pointing at a willow basket. It's full of bread and cheese and other food.

""""Gulp…""""

All of them gulp.

For the past few days, they've had nothing to eat but claylike provisions, making this simple basket look like a banquet.

"I'm not hallucinating, right…?"

"Ha-ha-ha-ha… A hot spring and banquet in middle of the forest? What kind of sick joke is this?"

The ranger grasps his cheeks and lets out a dry laugh.

Even if it's an illusion, they've stopped caring. They're past understanding at this point.

The ranger's laugh, which is closer to a sob by now, echoes into the forest.

He suddenly stops.

"…Nobody. Move," he warns.

The others look over to where the ranger is staring.

It's the unchanging forest thicket.

What could have gotten the ranger so worked up?

Just then, the clouds that were covering the moon shift.

There, reflected in the moonlight, are countless eyes.

"EEK…!"

How long have they been hiding there?!

Sure, they're tired, but even from this distance, they didn't sense anything.

Now they understand the strength of the creatures hidden in the woods.

They suddenly have the ominous feeling that a dragon, or some other legendary beast, is staring at them.

Ordinary adventurers wouldn't have noticed them.

But the guild's best high-class adventurers can tell the difference in their power.

They cannot win against whatever's in the brush.

The countless eyes hold no malice. But they are unsettling enough.

"...What is going on...?"

The captain has to swallow his fear to think.

Let's review the details.

Eyes watching them from the forest and the occasional flash of murderous intent. A hot-spring bath for cleaning the body. And a basket full of food.

What is the meaning behind all this?

"...Oh. I see now..."

The captain comes to a single conclusion.

"I get it. I have it now, you shapeless monsters. I know what you're after now."

He glares at the forest as he grits his teeth.

"We're your meal."

They prepare their meals by observing their prey, driving them to the edges of fear and exhaustion.

He's heard of vampires, intelligent monsters that improve the taste of their victim's blood by instilling them with fear.

The endless observation and hostile aura are all for the purpose of leading them here to be feasted upon.

And the final phase of the plan is to have the adventurers clean themselves in the hot spring and fatten themselves up with the food.

In response to the captain's conclusion, countless eyes seem to blaze in the darkness.

"Their meal...? Did you say we're their meal...?"

"Damn it all... We were playing right into their hands the whole time..."

Their bodies are frozen with fear.

Even if they head back now, it's too late. There's no way they would be able to return alive now that they know the truth.

The eyes in the thicket are just waiting for them to be done.

To go on is death. To turn back is death. The adventurers shout.

"Who… Who would happily go along with your plan?!"

"Do you think we're going to just let you eat us…?!"

"We're proud adventurers, the Swords of Dawn! Not some pigs to be eaten!"

"Let's go, men! We must complete this investigation no matter what. We'll go to the magic disaster point and report our findings to the guild! Even if only one of us survives, we shall emerge victorious!"

""""*Yeah!*""""

The adventurers, now fueled by rage, ignore the hot spring and food and run north for the waterfall.

† † †

""""…………""""

Whaaaaaaaaaaaat?!

The adventurers suddenly become enraged and run off.

"Arwf?! *(The hot spring! The feast! Aren't you going in?! Aren't you going to eat something?!)*"

I don't get it! What was wrong with the gift I put *all* my effort into?!

If it were me, I'd be over the moon to get in a bath and eat some good food. But it doesn't seem to appeal to the adventurers at all.

"Squee? *(More importantly, beloved, they're heading straight for the waterfall. Should we just leave them to it?)*"

"Arwf? *(Huh? The waterfall…? What about it…?)*"

I'm so shocked at my gift being ignored that I can't think about anything else.

What's wrong with them going there?

"Mrow. *(You know. The plan was to show them that there are no dangers in the forest while also slowing them down so that we could disperse the magic around the waterfall. Remember?)*"

"……Arwf. *(……Ah.)*"

"Squeak? *(……Don't tell me you forgot. What did you think we were going to do after this?)*"

"A-arwf. *(H-ha-ha-ha, whoops… Yeah, I completely forgot.)*"

"Mew… *(Routa…)*"

"Woof! *(S-stop it! Don't look at me like that!)*"

I look away from Nahura's judgmental stare.

"Squeak. *(Oh dear. So you're the type who turns the means into the goal and forgets about the future.)*"

Grrr. You're really enjoying this, aren't you?

But I have no comeback. Our main objective completely left my mind halfway through making the hot spring.

"Bark! *(N-no, we still have time!)*"

The treat failed, but we can still recover from this.

We just have to get to the waterfall before them and disperse the magic.

"Woof! *(Let's go! We're going to get there before the adventurers!)*"

"Grwl! *(Yes, sir! Leave the escort to us! You head there right away, my king!)*"

With a low growl, the Fen Wolves disperse.

Nahura and Len get on my back, and I run as fast as I can.

"Squee? *(By the way, darling, how do you plan on dispersing the magic?)*"

Len's question forces us to realize one crucial detail.

"Woof? *(Huh? Don't you two know?)*"

"Mew. *(I don't.)*"

"Squeak. *(Neither do I. I know how to use the magic within myself, but I have no idea how to disperse magic I've already released.)*"

What?!

Shouldn't that be your field of expertise as fantasy creatures?!

Just do some kind of *pow, pow, poof,* and it's gone, right?!

"Squeak. *(Weak humans have probably thought about how to use magic in the atmosphere. But dragons with an abundance of magic have no need for such things. We don't learn what we don't need to learn. That's just common sense, isn't it?)*"

"Woof! Woof! *(Don't act so high and mighty! What good is a thousand-year-old spinster?! A dragon who knows nothing is useless!)*"

"Squeak! *(Wh-what did you say?!)*"

"Woof! Woof! *(Which reminds me! You were completely useless this time, too! All you did was act arrogant and hang out on my head!)*"

"Meow! *(Oh, I helped out!)*"

"Woof! *(Yes you did! You're a good girl! Garo and others are good wolves! But, Len, you're a bad girl!)*"

A very bad girl! I won't forgive anyone who's an even bigger freeloader than I am!

"S-squeak! *(Wh-what?! If you're going to go that far, then just you wait! I'm going to show you how useful I can be!!)*"

And with that, Len flies into the air.

With a flash of light, a giant blue dragon appears.

"GROOOOOAR!! *(I just need to get there faster than them, right? When I put my mind to it, I can fly faster than the speed of sound!)*"

She grabs Nahura and me in her thick front claws.

"Bark! *(Hey! Wait! What if the adventurers see you?!)*"

Making them believe no monsters live here is a key part of the plan!

"GROOOOAR! *(It's fine! You males shouldn't split hairs! I just have to fly fast enough that they don't see me! Let us be off!!)*"

"Arwf! *(It's not fine! This isn't good at all! If you fly faster than the speed of sound, then you'll have to break the sound barri—)*"

We're suddenly struck with incredible speeds before I can finish.

Or so I think, but it doesn't happen.

I look down to the dark forest to see it whizzing past, but I don't feel the wind at all.

"GRRRAR! *(Who do you think I am?! I put up a shield before breakfast! At this speed, the darkness will also keep us hidden from the adventurers.)*"

"Mew…? *(Um, about the adventurers…you know when we just flew up into the air…?)*"

I look down to see that the adventurers, smaller than grains of rice, have fallen over on the riverbank.

They remind me of people I've seen get knocked over by typhoon winds.

Ohhh, they're gonna be all beat up… Yikes…

"……GROOOOAR! *(……Perfect! That will buy us some more time!)*"

"Woof… *(This is terrible. They're definitely going to think there's something wrong with this forest…)*"

Even if we get ahead of them, we have no way to disperse the magic. There's no way to fix this.

Checkmate. Total checkmate.

The adventurers are going to report everything to the guild. Then the real investigation will begin.

If loads of adventurers come, they'll find Garo and the other Fen Wolves and spread the word that this forest isn't safe.

And if loads of adventurers show up, at least one of them is bound to uncover my true identity.

Even the clueless people at the mansion will be swayed if a crowd of people explain it to them.

It's over! My pet life is over!

I hang limp in Len's claws as I lose all hope and the energy drains from my body.

Flying at that speed, it's barely a moment before Len arrives at the waterfall.

She beats her wings a few times to slow down, and we have a smooth landing.

"GRAR? *(Darling, we're here… Hey, what's the matter, darling?)*"

"Arww… *(Oh, you know. Just the realization that pet life as I know it is over, and there's no point in trying anymore…)*"

"GROOOAR? *(Hmph. What if we explain everything to them? I don't know much about these humans, but maybe they'll understand if you talk to them. Or shall I have a word with them?)*"

"Bark... *(Don't you remember what happened with Zenobia...? She attacked you before trying to talk to you...)*"

I lie down, drained of energy.

"GRRAR? *(Would you prefer we simply wait for something to be born of all the magic gathered here? A monster born of our magic would be a very powerful child. Then we can live a long life together as a family... Oh, that actually sounds like a great plan!)*"

"Woof! Woof! *(No it does not! How is it a solution to give the guild more monsters to hunt down?! Actually, can you please stop trying to force a kid on me?!)*"

What kind of messed up life plan ends with my being stuck with the responsibility of fatherhood as a two-month-old puppy?

"Arwf... *(Haah, it's no use...)*"

I won't be able to live at the mansion anymore once the cat's out of the bag.

Even if my lady and the others try to protect me, the guild will probably send adventurers to kill me.

Not low-level adventurers like this time, or hack adventurers like Zenobia, but a lot of really strong ones.

I'll have to leave the mansion before it becomes a battleground.

But then where will I go? A weak, city-spoiled child like me can't survive in the wilderness.

I'm scared of hunting, and I don't want to eat raw meat. Especially now that I've tasted old man James's cooking. Nothing else can even be considered food!

My life, my perfect doggy life, is over... All that awaits me is death by starvation...

Lady Mary, it looks like this is the end for your Routa.

Please be well...

"Mrow? *(Routa? Routa?)*"

Nahura pokes my nose with her long tail.

"...Woof. *(...What? I'm about to read my last will and testament. Don't get in the way.)*"

"Mewl! *(It looks like everything is okay now!)*"

"Arwf? *(Huh?)*"

I get up and look over to where Nahura is pointing.

"Oh my, you guys sure are late."

Over by the half-destroyed pool near the waterfall stands a witch with a silver staff.

She has silver hair, a wide-brimmed tricornered hat, long ears, and a voluptuous body.

She's a witch I know very well.

"Woof?! *(H-Hecate?! What are you doing here...?!)*"

I don't know if she's using her levitation magic or something, but she's standing on top of the water.

"Let's talk later. I've just finished the spell."

What spell?

As soon as she says that, she stabs her staff into the water. A giant, glowing magic circle causes the water to rise up with the staff in the center. It changes itself into complicated shapes as it expands all the way out to us.

"GRRAAR...?! *(Wh-what is this magic circle...?! I've never seen such a complicated spell before! I cannot decipher its purpose at all...!)*"

Looks like this magic confuses Len, even though she's lived for so long.

The giant magical circle becomes three-dimensional, and the light gets more intense.

"Woof?! *(Is it okay for us to be here?! Isn't this bad?!)*"

"Mew. *(Well, Mistress didn't say anything, so I suppose it's okay. She probably would have sent us off somewhere if we were in the way.)*"

Nahura, who knows Hecate the best, lazily plops down.

Hecate lets go of the staff stuck in the water and begins to chant in a way that sounds like she's singing.

As if in response to her chant, the shining magic circle covers the whole pool, and its pattern gets even more complicated.

"...Hmm, it might not be quite enough. Routa, over here, please."

"W-woof! *(Whoa, hey! What are you doing?!)*"

Hecate waves me over in the middle of her chant, and my body starts floating in the air. I float all the way over until I'm next to her.

"I was wondering if you might be able to add a little magic to my circle. It requires a bit more than I had expected."

"Woof! Woof?! *(We came here to get rid of the magic, but aren't you just adding to it?! Wait, what are you doing here in the first place?!)*"

"Now is not the time for explanations. But what if I told you that if you help me here, then all your problems up until now will be solved?"

"Woof! *(Seriously?! Then of course I'll help you!)*"

I don't know what she's going to do, but I'll do anything to protect my pet life!

"Thank you. If you could just hurl magic as hard as you can straight up, that would be great."

All right! Leave it to me. I just need to fire a beam straight up, right?

I'll just pack all my feelings into it, and here comes my vom-beam.

"Awoooooooooo?! *(Hey, adventurers, why didn't you want to get in my hot spriiiiiiiiiiing?!)*"

My howl of sorrow becomes a pillar of light, piercing right through the middle of the magic circle dome.

Or rather, the pillar of light crashes into the dome and splits off into six parts, which then diffuse down the walls of the dome, causing the circle to shine even brighter.

Like cogs in a machine, the complicated patterns of the magic circle begin to move faster, the light shining so bright it almost looks like daylight.

The white light illuminates all around me, and I'm forced to shut my eyes.

Just beyond my limited vision, I hear a *click* sound, as if a door just opened.

"That's one down," I hear Hecate murmur next to me, but her words are cryptic and strange.

"It's over. Good work, Routa."

I blink a few times as I open my eyes to see Hecate floating above the water.

The blinding magical circle that was just here has now completely vanished without a trace.

All that surrounds me is the glow of the moon and the sound of the waterfall.

"GRAAAR. *(Oh, the dense residual magic is gone.)*"

Dragon-mode Len lets out a long roar of admiration.

I can't sense it, but it seems what Len said is true.

"GROOOAR... *(Was it that magic circle? That seemed a bit excessive for the mere purpose of dispersing some magic... Rather than dispersing the magic, the circle seems to have converted it into something else...)*"

Len ponders the possibilities.

I'm also a little worried that something will come out of that magic circle, but so far, nothing.

"Arwf...? *(What* was *that...?)*"

That was an impressive display, but for everything to come to an end without anything happening is a blessing, if not a bit anticlimactic.

If this were a show at a theme park, everyone would have booed.

I can hear Hecate giggling as I pore over this.

"Hee-hee, it's a secret for now. But I know that someday it'll be something you'll find useful, Routa."

"Arwf...? *(Me...?)*"

Hecate, who's expression never falters, is covered in beads of sweat. Her breath is a little ragged, and her cheeks are flushed.

I guess that magic circle really did take a lot out of her.

"Arwf. *(Hmm, well, all right.)*"

I'll have no idea, even if I try to figure it out.

A pet dog doesn't need to know anything about magic. It's best to let sleeping thoughts lie.

"Woof! Woof! *(At least now all the residual magic is gone, right? Thanks, Hecate! I'm sure everything will be fine now!)*"

I'm pretty sure the adventurers can't see us.

And no matter how much they suspect, they won't get any proof.

If there's nothing wrong with the area they're supposed to investigate, then everything should be written off as the adventurers' hallucinations and baseless suspicions.

Okay, let's get out of here. Everyone, disperse.

Nahura, wake up. Len, hurry up and turn back into a mouse.

Just as I turn around to say that—Garo and the others run up to me.

"Grwl! *(Please forgive me, my king! We were unable to stop them from entering the magic circle!)*"

"Woof— *(Oh, hey, guys. Looks like things turned out okay in the end. The adventurers—)*"

"Grwl! *(—are almost here! You must hide yourselves, quickly!)*"

"Woof! Woof! *(Oh no! Hide, everyone! Hide now!)*"

"GROOAR… *(It would appear it's too late for that…)*"

Len points one of her claws over to where the four adventurers are standing.

"A-a dragon…?! That was what caused the strong wind before…?!"

"That's not all! Look at those ridiculously huge wolves! And isn't that white one from the mansion?! What's he doing here?! Were they the ones watching us this whole time…?!"

"What was that massive magic circle just now…?! That couldn't have been the work of humans…! Oh God…! I don't know what's what anymore…"

"No, what interests me more is that young lady!"

The adventurers are getting louder and louder, their rage increasing to the point where they're about to draw their weapons.

Haah, it's over. It's really over now.

They've seen Len in her dragon form—and the Fen Wolves frozen next to her. And with Hecate—sexy as ever—standing right there, she looks like an evil witch controlling all the monsters.

No matter how you look at it, we're a very suspicious group.

All that's left is to report it to the guild.

I just want to disappear.

"Hey, you were sent by the guild, correct?"

Hecate gives my dejected head a single pat as she steps forward.

"Hey! Stop right there, you suspicious witch!"

The leader takes the claymore off his back.

"I'm not going to do anything. There's nothing to be afraid of."

Hecate is unafraid of the sword as she steps forward.

"I—I said stop!"

"W-wait! Captain!"

It's the lancer who reins him in.

"Ah, it is! Now that I get a closer look, it really is!"

"What? She a friend of yours?"

The ranger looks at the lancer suspiciously.

"Not exactly, but everyone should know her! You know, the portrait up in the guild's headquarters!"

"But that painting is of the former guild master..."

"She's the founder! So the rumors that she's still alive and sometimes visits the current guild master are true!"

Hecate's the guild's founder?

That's a new development.

She's an incredible witch and an amazing doctor, she's higher in the pecking order than Papa, and now she's the founding guild master?

Who in the world are you, Hecate?

I don't know how long the guild's been around, but I feel like it's an organization with a long history.

Wait, so how old is she *really*?

"..............."

Ah. Did it just get colder?!

I just noticed her eyes have narrowed, and now she's looking at me.

Scary! Her wordless smile is emitting such murderous intent!

Any inquiry into age is bad. I'll remember that.

"...Excuse me, but may I have your name?"

The claymore-wielding leader directs the question to Hecate.

"Hecate Luluarus. I'm sorry to say I am still very much alive."

The lancer realizes how rude he was and quickly claps his hand over his mouth.

"Your name and appearance are the same as the portrait's— No, you're more beautiful in person… Your fame precedes you. Even cowardly adventurers like ourselves have heard of you. Please excuse our rudeness."

Their leader apologizes like a knight.

"But if you are the founder of the guild, then what are you doing here?"

The ranger turns his suspecting gaze to her.

His eyes look like they won't yield to any authority.

"Sorry about that. I was just doing a little magic experiment. But everything's fine now. It's all over and done with. Look at your device. It's not reacting to any magic, is it?"

"Huh, that's impossible…… You're kidding. All traces of magic have completely disappeared."

The ranger with the device is speechless.

"I'm sure that even if we ask about this experiment of yours, we won't understand, so I won't ask, but…what about those monsters?"

"These are all my friends."

"So they're your familiars…? But I can't believe you'd have a dragon familiar… No, that's possible for someone like you."

Hecate smiles, neither denying nor acknowledging his statements.

So she's a schemer who prefers to let someone misunderstand a situation.

"GRAR…? *(Who are you calling a familiar…?)*"

"Woof! *(Shh. This is going well—don't interrupt! Stay! Staaaay!)*"

"GRR…? *(I know that. Who do you think I am, darling…?)*"

Len only growled a little, but I can sense the adventurers start to tremble.

Not as bad as Zenobia, but pretty close.

"Th-then the ones watching us were these monsters?"

The priest asks the question in utter fear.

"Watching? Oh, sorry. These children seemed to have made a mistake. Please let me apologize on their behalf. I would be most grateful if you would tone that part down in your report to the guild. If you need a witness for your report, I'd be happy to answer a summons."

Hecate manages to thwart all the adventurers' questions before they're able to ask them.

"Hmm, really… One more thing, though. Does Marquis Faulks, the owner of these lands, know you're in these woods…?"

"Of course he does. It seems that piece of information didn't make it to you."

"Really? …Then there isn't a problem here."

They'd been made to come all this way just for this, and while they may feel there's an issue, they won't raise a fuss over it. These adventurers are professionals, after all.

The founder of the guild says there's no problem, and in the end, any further questioning should be conducted by their superior. And Hecate says she'd answer a summons.

There's nothing the adventurers can do right now.

Just as Hecate promised, everything is resolved.

"It seems you've endured something horrible on your way here. I hope you can take it easy when you get back. Make sure you tell the guild master that your mission has been completed."

Hecate waves her staff, and a white light glows under the adventurers' feet.

It's the teleportation magic we've seen many times.

"Wh-what?! Is this—?"

She doesn't show any consideration to them as they all scream, eyes wide, then vanish.

"Woof? *(Hmm, that's the fastest I've ever seen someone get rid of troublesome people. Where did you send them?)*"

"To the front of the gate of the Royal Capital. It would cause an uproar if they suddenly appeared in the middle of the guild headquarters."

Well, I'm sure the people you just sent away will be in an uproar themselves.

As well as anyone at the gate who happens to see them magically appear.

"Woof? *(So wait. Does that mean this ordeal is finally over?)*"

"Mew. *(Looks like it. Feels a bit anticlimactic.)*"

"GRAAR. *(Hmm. Perhaps if we'd asked the Lady Witch right from the start, this would have been over a lot sooner.)*"

Don't say that. You're going to make me regret everything.

I had made a new resolution when I was reborn. I promised myself I would mooch off the hard work of others whenever possible. But once again, I ended up doing honest work.

This is completely inappropriate behavior for a no-good freeloading hound. This just proves that working yourself to the bone is *never* worth it.

"Oh my, that is a problem."

"Arwf? *(What's a problem?)*"

"That hot spring you put so much effort into making is going to waste."

"Bark? *(Huh? You want to try it?)*"

Wait, how does she know about that? I think for a second, but then I remember she's connected to Nahura's eyes and ears.

"Yes, of course I'll use it. You worked so hard for this, after all."

Oh right, Hecate loves baths. Or rather, she *loves* drinking in the bath.

Ah, I can see it now.

I can see one of Papa's special-reserve wines waiting for us.

"And of course, she'll need a clean, too."

I look down to see Nahura lazily grooming herself.

Her face jolts up from everyone watching her.

"Mewl? *(U-um, Mistress? Why do I have a really bad feeling right now…?")*

"I told you to say 'meow' at the ends of your sentences, didn't I?

This calls for punishment. I'm going to be even rougher than usual when scrubbing you."

"Gyeow! *(N-no punishmeeeent! No baaaaaaaath!)*"

Hecate grabs Nahura by the scruff of the neck as she tries to run away, then casts her teleportation magic.

Suddenly, we're back at the hot spring.

"Now then, it's bath time. I really worked up a sweat, so I'm sure the liquor will taste divine."

"Gyeeoow! *(Not a baaath! Not a baaaaaaaath!)*"

"GRRAR. *(I see—so that is hot water for bathing… Then it is time for my secret plan.)*"

"Woof. *(Why are you making that face? Hurry up and turn back into a mouse.)*"

"GRAR! *(I will not! For this is my true form!)*"

We're arguing back and forth like always when suddenly, everything turns white with a burst of space-time magic.

Here I am, thinking we'd just been wasting our time, but this whole uproar has been wrapped up neatly with a nice little bow.

And they all live happily ever after.

…Right?

Epilogue

"Arwwww… *(Aaaaahhhh…)*"

Whoa. I really sound like an old man.

"Arwf… *(But I can't help it; this is the beeeest…)*"

As I sink my humongous body into the hot water, it rises up and spills over the rocky edge.

My fluffy fur spreads out, and the feeling of the hot-spring water seeping into it feels incredibly good.

I look up at the half-moon shaped like a fluffy omelet. The white steam drifts upward, and the water's surface glistens in the moonlight.

Well, I have to say bathing in a hot spring on a moonlit night sure is fancy.

When I bathe with Lady Mary, she always jumps on me, and I swim around like a steamboat, but tonight is a special treat just for adults.

I can just relax and enjoy the hot spring.

It's a shame the adventurers went back without trying it. Their loss.

I asked Garo and some of the others if they wanted to join, but she said no and that she was worried about neglecting the protection of the forest for so long because they were escorting the adventurers.

They must have been exhausted, but they ran off gallantly into the forest so quickly that I couldn't tell.

Hmm, Fen Wolves sure are workaholics. I really am a disgrace to Fen Wolf–kind!

But I don't care! I'm the king! Who's gonna say anything?

It's too bad Garo and the others didn't want to join, but it's not like this hot spring is going anywhere. I can just invite them later.

Heh-heh-heh, no one can resist once they find out how good this feels. They won't get away next time.

"This really is an exquisite bath..."

The person who teleported the adventurers (who were originally supposed to be in the spring right now) to town lets out a big sigh.

Hecate soaks in the waters next to me.

She stretches her arms and back to alleviate stiffness.

Her stark-naked body is a sight to behold. And once again, her cups runneth over. I can't stress this enough. She truly is blessed.

"Mreooow... *(I don't want any more baaaaaaaaths...)*," says Nahura, who has been forced into the bath and now lies exhausted on Hecate's chest.

Nahura hates baths, so she can't appreciate how truly wonderful this hot spring is. It's just so sad.

But that makes me realize something amazing.

"Woof......! *(Oh...... They're floating. Look at them float......!)*"

Nahura's weight causes Hecate's large breasts to bob up and down.

They're so big, she could probably balance anything on them.

"Woof... *(I could really go for a beer right now...)*"

Drinking alcohol after a bath is the best, but drinking while in a piping-hot hot spring is also pretty good.

In the winter, you drink sake, but for summer, you've gotta have beer.

"Oh my. I might just have some, actually."

"Woof?! *(Huh? Really?!)*"

Hecate waves her index finger around in a circle.

A hole in the air opens up, and a ceramic bottle and a cup fall out.

"This is ale. It's different from lager because it doesn't have any hops in it."

She pours an amber liquid into the cup as she talks.

A nice thin layer of foam rises to the top, and droplets of condensation begin to drip down the side of the cup.

"Arwf...arwf...! *(Ohhhh, it's ice-cold...!)*"

"Tee-hee."

Hecate giggles as I reel in my drool, and she places the almost-overflowing cup against her lips.

"Glug, glug."

Her slender throat moves seductively as she downs the whole thing, sounding very satisfied as she does.

"Phew... Delicious..."

She licks the foam off her lips and sighs.

That alluring figure—I can't take it anymore!

"Woof! Woof! *(I want some! Gimme! Gimme!)*"

I'm a sucker for beer commercials. My current view is so much better than a commercial that my desire to purchase a drink is overwhelming. If this aired on TV, I'd immediately buy an entire crate.

Which reminds me, she probably swiped this beer from the mansion! As a member of the Faulks family, I have a right to drink it!

Gimme! Gimme some beer!

"Hee-hee-hee, do you want to do *that* again?"

She takes her hand out of the water and is about to pour the drink down her fingertips.

"Woof! Woof! *(You'll get the water dirty if you do that here! And you're not supposed to get the towel in the water! Hmph!)*"

As someone who's whole body looks like a towel, what am I saying...? This isn't the time for that sort of critique.

"Arwf? *(Huh? That reminds me, where did Len run off to?)*"

She normally makes some kind of snide remark from the top of my head right about now. But she doesn't seem to be there, nor anywhere in my mane.

She's on my back 24-7, so it's strange that she's not there for once.

"Woof! *(Hmm, oh well. More importantly, beer! Please give me the glorious beer!)*"

I stick my face into the freshly poured cup and gulp the ale down.

"Arwf…! *(Oh, oh yeeeesssss…!)*"

There's barely any bitterness, and a carbonated sweet fruitiness runs down my throat.

The flavor is completely different from beer in the other world.

The fizziness isn't strong, but it has the full-bodied fragrance of squeezed fruit. The aftertaste is like freshly baked bread. Its richness fills my empty belly.

This isn't a drink you gulp down, but one where you savor the taste on your tongue.

"Woof, woof! *(Hmm, not like that's going to stop me, though!)*"

Let's gulp this down! Everyone has their own way of drinking!

"Oh my, you drink well. How about some snacks?"

"Garwf, garwf. *(Oh, so good—ham on bread would go great with this!)*"

That sounds so good. So delicious.

With the snacks and ale Hecate is providing, the hot spring is made perfect.

The beer is delicious. The hot spring feels amazing……

Right! This is the paradise *we* created…!

"Mwa-ha-ha! Oh, darling. If you require someone to pour drinks for you, then just ask me."

Oh, looks like Len's finally arrived.

"Woof…? *(How do you expect to pour anything with a body like yours…?)*"

It's an impossible task for a dragon or a mouse.

It'll either be too heavy and she'll drop it, or she'll put too much strength into it and break it. Either way, I can only imagine the bottle shattering.

Wait a second… Did she just speak normally…?

I think this over as I turn around and see a completely naked young lady.

"Arwf…? *(It can't be… Is that you, Len?)*"

"Indeed."

She nods. She's not embarrassed by her naked body at all and is, in fact, standing proud as she pops into the hot spring and snuggles up next to me.

"I realized something. If you are excited by young human women, then I must assume the form of a human."

Well, Len nodding in her new form sure is something.

Her shoulder-length hair is a luscious black. Her sharp eyes are red like fire. And her skin is as white as snow.

Now that I take a closer look, she has what appear to be horns sticking out from either side of her head. Her nails look sharp, and she has a short, scaly tail coming out from the bottom of her spine.

The finer details are a little strange here and there, but she has transformed herself into a very cute girl.

"This took a lot of work. I really can't tell the difference between humans. It took a long time to practice getting this body just right."

Len keeps shooting me seductive glances as she stokes my chin with her slender fingers.

"What do you think? Does it make you want to mate with me right now? Does it make you desire lots of descendants?"

"Arwf. *(Nope, not at all.)*"

"What?!"

Her eyes widen at my immediate response.

"Wh-why not…?! This is the kind of female you lust after, you pervert! How are you not excited by this form?!"

"Woof! Woof! *(Who are you calling a pervert?! Rude! Besides, you look* way *too young! I'm not a pedophile!)*"

Len does look cute, but she also looks like she's five or six years old.

Plus, she's *completely* flat.

More like an infant than a child. I want to dress her up in a smock.

"Wh-what?! But are you not always fawning over the young females in the mansion? The younger the better, right?!"

"Woof… *(I feel like there's been a* grave *misunderstanding…)*"

I howl at the clueless spinster from my position in the bath.

"Woof! Woof! *(And besides, this Routa is not some irresponsible pet who would have puppies without his owner's permission!)*"

I don't want to get castrated! No way!

"Woof! Woof! *(I live without a lick of worldly obligations or responsibility. I get petted all the time, and I love being lazy. I'm proud of that!)*"

Len's eyes snap wide as she realizes the truth.

"O-oh… So my secret plan…"

Tears stream down Len's face as she sinks under the water, blowing bubbles.

"No matter how important you try to make it seem, it just wasn't that noble a goal…"

Hecate watches us as she drinks her beer in shock.

"U-uwah… Why did I even try so hard…? I had to not only prepare the spell but imagine a new human form, and now I have to forget it again… Do you have any idea how long it takes…?"

"Woof! Woof? *(No biggie! Want a beer?)*"

"You jerk!"

Len readies her claws as she launches herself at me.

"It's a wife's job to look after her terrible husband! You're a pervert, and now you've dragged me down with you! We're in this together, so I'm making you accept your hand in all this!!"

"W-woof! Woof! *(H-hey, wait, nooooooooooo!! Y-you'll make me uncleeeeaaaan!!)*"

"My, oh my. Well, now."

Hecate watches the aggressive Len and the submissive me, her hand raised to her mouth as if watching a sport.

"Woof! *(Hey! Don't just watch! Help!)*"

"I don't think so. I decided I would never get involved with someone who's head over heels."

"Woof! Woof! *(Then, Nahura! Nahura! You'll do! Help me out here!)*"

I plead to Nahura, who's still lying on Hecate's chest with vacant eyes.

"Mewl. *(Did you save me when Mistress was torturing me, Routa? Did you not laugh? ... Which means that's just how it is.)*"

"Kya-ha-ha! You have no one to back you up, darling! Prepare yourself!!"

"Arwwww!! *(N-noooooooooooooo!! I don't want to be a two-month-old daaaaaad!!)*"

With a gentle breeze, the moonlit hot spring is plunged into chaos.

Thankfully, I am able to defend my virginity.

† † †

"Mewl. *(Goodness me, what a disaster, Routa.)*"

"Arwf... *(You... I'll remember this...)*"

"Meow. *(Why? You reap what you sow. Lady Len loves you dearly, and yet, all you do is give her the cold shoulder. Of course that would happen.)*"

I got out of the bath and am now lying on top of a giant boulder, my body stretched out and cooling.

The cool boulder feels good on the stinging bites covering my body.

"Woof... *(I wasn't unreasonable. I've just been telling her how I really feel...)*"

"Mew, mew? *(Sometimes white lies are necessary. Don't you think it'll be great? Having lots of little children? I'm sure Len would be a great mother.)*"

"Woof! Woof! *(I've already told you I'm not a furry, and I'm certainly not some dragon pedophile! I was surprised she transformed herself into a human, but still...)*"

A spinster's tenacity is terrifying.

If she hadn't made herself look so young and added another ten years *at least*, I may have fallen for her.

But not only did she become a child, but we're still different species. What could we do about that?

Do monsters often crossbreed?

Well, it has nothing to do with someone like me who's committed, body and soul, to the pet life.

If more cute, fluffy puppies appeared, then my lady's affections would be taken from me. The only one she needs to pamper is me.

"Arwf… *(Haah, I feel exhausted from everything that's happened…)*"

I rest my chin on my forepaws.

Why am I this tired from being in a revitalizing hot spring?

I just want to live my stress-free pet life.

How contradictory is that?

Luckily, everything was handled thanks to Hecate. I was able to protect my pleasant pet life.

I don't really know what that giant magical circle was, nor do I understand what Hecate did in the end.

"Mewl. *(All right then, I'll give Routa a special cat massage as a present. How's that?)*"

Nahura climbs onto my tired back and massages me, alternating her front paws.

"Arwf… *(Ahhhh… I may be biased, but this is the best…)*"

"Mewl. *(Paw, paw, rub, rub.)*"

The feeling of her soft paws working into my back feels amazing.

Ahhh, I feel so much better.

Below the boulder I'm being massaged on, Len is sulking, and Hecate is right next to her. They're drinking and talking about something.

"Pfaah! That hit the spot!"

I'm sure they don't care, but it's normally illegal for a young girl to gulp down alcohol and sigh like that. Then again, she's a thousand-year-old spinster on the inside, so I guess it's fine.

Being a furry with a thing for young boys means she's more like a pedophilic thousand-year-old spinster… I kind of feel bad for her…

Urgh, now she's crying again.

"Miss Witch…my darling…I don't know what you're plotting, but…as my husband…"

"It's unfortunate… I'm sure you'll… I'll…someday…"

It's hard to hear over the waterfall in the hot spring. I hear "husband" but not much else. If I can't hear it, then I can't hear it.

Either way, it sounds like they're complaining about me.

Worthless. Pervert. Lick-o-phile.

Sniff.

Whatever, I'll just have my lady compliment me. She'll squish my cheeks.

"Mewl. *(I can sense you're terrible from the ground up. How interesting.)*"

"Bark, bark! *(Ha-ha-ha. That's because I'm aiming to be the world's most worthless dog!)*"

Lady Mary is happy to pet me. I'm happy being petted.

It's an easy relationship we both get pleasure from. That's a pet and master for you.

A pet's job is to be spoiled. A pet who works isn't a pet at all.

I'm a dog who takes great pride in his life as a pet. I'm the ideal pet, aren't I?

"Woof, woof?! *(Don't you think so, Nahura?!)*"

"Meow. *(I don't know what you're talking about, but I do know you're a terrible creature.)*"

"Woof, woof? *(Yes, true, but could you try praising me a little more?)*"

"Meow. *(Ha-ha-ha, oh, Routa. Who's a good boy?)*"

Our laughs echo in the moonlit night.

† † †

"Squee…? *(Why…*hic… *Why, my darling…*hic…*will you not embrace me…?* …Hic…?*)*"

Len's drunk on my back, and I'm standing in the garden.

I had managed to convince her to turn back into a mouse, but it was a lot of work.

"Woof, woof! *(We're good friends!)*"

"Squee! Squee! *(Noooo! Breed with me! Darling is a horrible pervert, so just follow those natural inclinations and let's make one or two new little lives!)*"

"Woof, woof! *(Who are you calling a horrible pervert?! I'm just a nice guy who's interested in a wide variety of people!)*"

"Squeak! *(That means you're just not interested in me! We may be different species, but we're both monsters!)*"

"Woof, woof! *(I already told you—I'm not a furry!)*"

"Squeak, squeak!! *(But humans are further from yoooouuuu! You disgusting perveeeeerrrrt!!)*"

After screaming, Len suddenly calms down.

"Squeak… *(Ugh, can you walk a bit quieter, beloved…? I think I'm going to… Oh, could this be morning sickness…?!)*"

"Woof. *(Ugh, damn spinster. You* reek *of thousand-year-old spinster…)*"

I give up with a sigh and turn around.

"See you later, Routa. That was a lot of fun."

Hecate, who brought us back with her space magic, holds up her long skirt in one hand and her wide-brimmed hat in the other and curtsies.

"Woof! *(Yeah! Later!)*"

"Mewl! *(Let me know if you ever want another cat massage!)*"

Nahura waves a paw from her perch on Hecate's shoulder.

"Woof? *(What's it gonna cost me?)*"

"Mewl! *(Just your time!)*"

"Woof! *(That's ominous!)*"

What would she make me do?!

The space around Hecate's feet glows, and the two of them seem to fade away, then vanish.

"Woof. *(All right then, let's head home and hop back into bed. My lady is waiting.)*"

"Squee… *(Why that little girl…? I'm the better woman…)*"

You're even younger than she is when you turn human.

No, even mentally, my lady is more mature than you…

How did this spinster survive for a thousand years?

I leave Len curled up in a ball on my head and head back into the mansion from the back door of the kitchen.

Passing through, I decide to check on the old man asleep at his recipe-covered desk. As always, I grab a blanket from the linen room and pull it over him.

"Mmm…?"

Uh-oh, he's waking up.

"Hmm…? Oh, it's you, Routa. I'm guessing you're stealing again?"

He grins at me and stretches.

The blanket around his shoulders falls to the floor.

"Oh, so it was you who's been putting a blanket on me… What a clever boy."

He says thank you by ruffling my head with his burly hand.

"Woof, woof! *(No problem! It's great that you're passionate about your work, but you should really get a good night's sleep in a bed!)*"

As I reply, my tail wags with a *whm, whm.*

"I know, I know. I'll go sleep in my room. You should keep the midnight play to a minimum and get back to the young lady."

Did my thoughts reach him? He lights the lantern, and we leave the room.

Eventually, we part ways, and I head up the stairs to Lady Mary's room.

I stand up on my hind legs and use my forepaws to open the door.

The bedroom is incredibly quiet. All I can hear is my lady's even breaths.

I take great care not to wake her as I sneak back under the duvet. My head pops out right next to her face.

Oh, crap, the bed's creaking.

"Ghnn… Routa…"

Lady Mary hugs me like always, rubs her face in my fur, then falls asleep again.

I feel like the day isn't over if I don't see her sleeping face at least once.

"Arww. *(But still, today was a* really *long day.)*"

I wriggle my head to prepare my own pillow.

"Squea… *(Darling…I'll never give up…)*"

"Woof, woof. *(Yeah, yeah.)*"

I admire her determination.

I admire it, but I don't accept it!

Now then, tomorrow it's back to the life of a lazy pet.

Spending every day just eating and sleeping is wonderful. I feel like I'll have a good dream tonight.

Good night.

It's been a few days since that night.

Today is another day I'm spending my time peacefully at the Faulks mansion.

I'm doing the same thing I do every day, eating delicious food and sleeping as much as I like.

My lady spoils me, and I help Toa with the laundry and run away whenever Zenobia tests her new blades… I guess that last part isn't exactly peaceful.

Either way, ever since we got rid of those adventurers, no major issues have occurred.

Even now, I'm having a rest over by the tables in the garden.

Lady Mary, with a tea set beside her, turns a page in her book. It's a faint sound but one of my little pleasures in life.

That's when Hecate shows up.

"Pardon my intrusion."

Miranda quickly prepares tea for the witch who selfishly invites herself over as if this were her own home.

"Oh! Dr. Hecate!"

My lady is thrilled. She leaps up out of her chair and throws herself into Hecate's arms.

"Arrrwn. *(You've been over a lot lately.)*"

I yawn and scratch the back of my ear with my leg as I look at her.

"Oh my, have I been too much of a nuisance?"

Nope, not at all. It's just that every time you're here, Papa's liquor collection gets smaller and smaller. It's really sad… Then again, you always let me have some, too!

"I'm so happy you're here, Doctor! You never came that often before…"

Before Lady Mary's illness was cured.

It was an incredibly rare and painful disease where once a year she'd get a month-long fever.

It was hard watching her suffer like that. But we don't need to worry about that anymore.

She's all cured thanks to the medicinal plant we got for her and Hecate turning it into a miracle drug.

"You're such a good girl, Mary. In fact, I have a gift to reward you for always behaving."

"Huh? Really?!"

She claps her hands together, and her eyes light up with expectation.

"Then again, I suppose it would be more accurate to say I have a gift for Routa."

With that, Hecate takes out a beige box using her space magic.

It's a shallow wooden box that looks like it might contain cookies, but I wonder what's really inside.

I peek over from the side, and my lady lifts the lid.

"Oh! Woooow, how pretty…!"

She takes out a dazzling belt that makes our eyes shine.

Intricate silver patterns are engraved into the red leather. The center is adorned with a beautiful gem.

"Arwf…? *(Is this…?)*"

"It's a collar for Routa!"

Hecate smiles and nods.

Oh yeah, I haven't had a collar this whole time. The one we bought in the Royal Capital flew off when I howled.

I have fixed my relationship with Toa, but I can tell other servants are still scared of my ever-growing body.

I was just thinking about how it was probably because I couldn't get ahold of another collar to improve my image.

I guess Hecate remembered what happened at the pet shop. And she got me this wonderful collar.

I have no choice but to accept it.

"Thank you so much, Dr. Hecate!"

My lady thanks her and begins to put it around my neck.

That's when a small shadow leaps out of my mane to block it.

"Squeak!! *(Stop, my darling!! Don't put it on!!)*"

"Arwf?! *(Huh?!)*"

Len leaps onto the top of my head and squeaks alarmingly, fur standing on end.

"Squeak! *(That isn't any ordinary collar! The technique is too complicated for me to read, but an incredibly strong magic has been carved into the design! That collar's been enchanted!)*"

The moment she says "enchanted," I think of the brainwashed monsters at Drills's house.

Len suspects this collar might be enchanted with something similar.

"Squeak! *(Remember the magic circle at the waterfall? This witch's actions are incredibly suspicious. I'm certain she's up to no good!)*"

"Hee-hee. You're right. It's very suspicious."

Hecate shoots us an evil grin.

"What do you think, Routa? Would you accept a gift from a wit—?"

"Woof! Woof! *(I accept! I'll put it on! I'll put it on right now! Yes, my lady! On! On!)*"

My tail wags like crazy as I urge Lady Mary to put the collar on me.

"Hey, you need to keep still, or I won't be able to put it on."

"Squea…! *(Darling! What about my warn—?)*"

Yeah, yeah, hush now.

I push the squeaking Len back down into my fur.

Hecate looks at me with a dark expression as I do that.

"…You don't suspect me at all?"

"Arwf. *(Nope.)*"

I've known for a long time now that Hecate's someone I can trust.

She probably never came to the mansion that much until Lady Mary's illness was cured because she was looking for the medicine.

Not to mention, those drugs couldn't be found anywhere. It was also difficult to find a dragon's nest where the ingredients for the medicine grew. I can't believe she found the time to do that.

If she hadn't looked for it beforehand, she wouldn't have been able to tell me about it.

This situation in the forest earlier is the same. It was Hecate who cleared away the magical residue as well as the adventurers' suspicions.

She seems suspicious and says cryptic things, but she's always had our best interests at heart.

I'm not suspicious of her at all.

"…………"

It doesn't matter what kind of magic this collar has on it. It won't bring us any misfortune. I'm sure of it.

Also. Including my life in the other world, this is the first time I've received a present from a friend. I'm super-happy.

"Woof! *(Thank you, Hecate. I'll take good care of it!)*"

"…Honestly, teasing you doesn't work at all."

She lets out a dejected sigh.

"Mew. *(You say that, but your ears are bright red, Mistress Hecate. You should just be honest and say you're happy that Routa believes in you— Gyah?!)*"

"Silence……!"

Nahura says too much again and gets stomped on.

With the affectionate eyes of a master watching over their pet, my lady finishes putting the collar on me.

"There you go, Routa."

"Woof! Woof! *(Sweet! Well? How does it look? Does it suit me?)*"

"It's wonderful, Routa."

The collar shines on my neck.

The soft tanned collar around my neck isn't tight at all. I can tell she invested a lot of time and care making it for me.

I'm so happy. I'm really excited now.

"Woof! Woof! *(All right! I don't have anything to give you in return, but we can at least go for a walk!)*"

"Oh my, shall I add a leash?"

"Arwf! *(Fwa-ha-ha! No need! Here!)*"

I run behind Hecate and push her from behind so her knees buckle, and suddenly, she's sitting on my back.

"H-hey, wait! Routa?!"

I dash through the garden with a panicked Hecate on my back.

"Woof! Woof! *(Hey, hey, miss! Wanna go play by the lake?)*"

"Oh honestly, Routa… Very well. I'll go on a date with you."

She holds down her wide-brimmed hat and beams a glorious smile.

"Arwf?! *(Huh?! A-a date?! No, I wasn't thinking of something so grand like that… I just wanted to say thank you…)*"

"Mrow. *(It's just like Routa to be flustered over something like that.)*"

"Squeak! *(What is the meaning of this? And to think, you were treating* me *like the villain for worrying. In that case, I won't forgive you for cheating!)*"

"Arww?! *(Ow?!)*"

She bites my head, which causes me to buck like a rodeo bull.

"Eek?! H-honestly!"

Hecate's surprised, but she also seems to be enjoying herself. She laughs as she clings to my neck. This is the first time I've seen her laughing innocently like a child.

I like this a lot more than the mischievous grin she usually wears.

"That's no fair, Doctor! I want to go, too!"

Oh, whoops. We left Lady Mary behind.

"No need to worry. You shan't be left behind."

Miranda solemnly takes my lady's hand.

"I've made all the necessary preparations! Get in!"

Zenobia, sitting in the driver's seat of the carriage, pulls up right next to them.

"Now then, let's go, everyone!"

My lady issues her command from the carriage, pointing straight ahead at me, and the horses neigh and begin to canter.

Another peaceful, lively, fun day begins.

Afterword

Hello, good evening, and good night. This is Inumajin.

I'm thrilled I get to see you again with the second volume.

Fantastic! The second volume is out! It's really thanks to everyone who purchased the first book! Thank you so much!! I'm working hard to continue writing the series at this rate, so I hope you'll enjoy what comes next!

By the way, I'm writing this afterword in January, so it's freezing cold in Kansai. I'm shivering every single day. It's too cold to go outside. I'm worried the drains have all frozen. I hope it's a lot warmer when you buy this book.

Take care not to catch a cold! Not like me! *Cough!*

And now I have some important news!

The *Woof Woof Story* manga has just begun!

The Japanese online manga website ComicWalker is releasing a chapter every month online for free, so I hope you'll check it out.

The artist Koikura kiki is able to show a different fun side to Routa and Lady Mary.

Be prepared for *even more* food porn than the novel. I drooled so much when I was reading the manga.

Sautéed veal… Trout *poêlé*… The wild boar covered in a thick layer of cheese… *Drool…*

* * *

I don't have much space left, so I'll end with my thanks.

To Kochimo, who has illustrated such beautiful and cute images for the novel. My editor, K, who continues to work with me even now. Koikura kiki, who's making such a fantastic manga. My senior and rival, Juichi Yasui. All the editors and my designer, proofreader, marketer, all the booksellers. Aaaand YOU!

I owe you all so much! I hope to see you all for the next volume! Later, then!

2018.1 Inumajin